FATED

A Prophecies of Angels and Demon Novellas

Book .5

CASSANDRA ASTON

For every girl whose rage could burn the world. And for Trisha. I wrote this one for you.

CONTENTS

CONTENT & TRIGGER WARNING

F ated is a work of fiction. No part of the book should be construed as true or accurate; no people or animals were harmed in the creation of this story. This series is intended for mature readers and is recommended for 18+. Mature content and triggers for the series are listed below.

Descriptions of torture and death

Allusions to rape and other acts of sexual deviance

Necromancy and reincarnation

Biblical and other related references

References to angels, demons, heaven, hell, and consequences for human actions

Explicit language and behavior as well as some open-door scenes depicting sexual acts

Witches, magic, and other magical, fantastical beings

Potentially inaccurate descriptions of periods in history

Feelings of desire, carnal and otherwise—for demonic creatures, may ensue – You've been warned

BOOKS BY CASSANDRA ASTON

Prophecies of Angels and Demons

Grave Secrets – book 1
Firefly – Simon's Novella – book 1.5
Grave Prophecies – book 2
Light – Gabriel's Novella – book 2.5
Grave Revelations – book 3
Fated – Sanura's Novella – book .5
Parable – Peter's Novella – book 3.5

Deadly Fae Duology

Whispers Among Thorns – Coming June 2025
Book 2 – Coming December 2025

Vicious Villains: A Twisted Fairytale Reimagining Anthology Series

Book 1 – Coming 2026

CASSANDRA ASTON

CHAPTER 1

Sanura

S anura ran her comb through mahogany curls that fell in ringlets down her back, hints of gold catching in the flickering candlelight.

"Sanura?"

Shalim stepped on light feet into her room, glancing around the space. "Please, Sanura, tell me you've finished packing your things."

Sanura glanced at her half-filled sack resting against the far wall and bit her lip. "Must I go, Mother?"

Shalim knelt before her, holding out a hand.

Sanura rested the comb in her palm and turned around, staring at the wall.

Her mother dipped two fingers into the oil pot beside her bed and rubbed Sanura's scalp. "My darling. Your gifts have grown beyond our coven's ability." She ran the comb through her hair, brushing each section before plaiting it into a braid. "Your uncle has secured a place for you in the coven of Gavras in Athens. With them, you will learn to harness this great power inside you."

Sanura's throat was dry and the words cracked when she twisted around, locking eyes with her mother. "But I don't want to leave you and Father."

Shalim tsked, motioning her daughter to turn her head. She did, sniffling softly.

When Shalim had finished, Sanura faced her mother as she wrapped a shawl over her plaited hair and set the comb down on the stone table.

Sanura's vision blurred. "It's so far away."

Her mother chuckled. "Would you rather stay with the goats and chickens? Athens is a beautiful city full of culture and life. Go, learn from the witches. Perhaps one day, you will bring your gifts back and bless us all."

A knock sounded at the entrance to their home, and both Sanura and Shalim looked up. Her father rose from his place in the corner and shuffled through their arched door and out of sight.

"My king," her father said. The women hurried to stand as a man in grand robes stepped into the room.

Shalim strode forward, bowing her head to kiss the rings at his knuckles, and Sanura followed, bending at the waist.

Imposing guards flanked him on either side. They stood almost a head above their king, bronze breastplates strapped over their broad chests, pressing massive spears into the dirt.

From her vantage point, Sanura studied the feet of the man on her right: he wore sandals laced up his calves. They were modern and drew the eye to tanned, thickly muscled legs. Her gaze trailed up, halting at the edge of his chiton, wondering for a moment what the rest of his muscled thigh must look like.

"Sanura," her mother hissed, drawing her focus back to the more important man in their home—the king.

She straightened, meeting his eyes for a moment before dropping her gaze. "My king."

He gave her an appraising stare. "This is the Witch of Endor? She's hardly more than a girl."

Her father tipped a finger under her chin, lifting her gaze once more to the king.

Sanura's bright golden eyes met the king's, and she gasped, stumbling backward as he dropped to the dirt floor before her. "Please. If what they say is true, I beg you. I seek the counsel of a great king. I am told you can help me."

She glanced at her mother, who gave her a nod of encouragement. Sanura stared at the man's bowed head, swallowing.

He remained on his knees, waiting.

Steeling herself, she cleared her throat. "I will help you. Tell me where your king is buried, and I will call on him."

King Saul and ten men, each twice her size, led Sanura to a small chariot pulled by two speckled mares. Sanura stopped beside the first, holding up her hand. The mare's soft snout blew warm breath across her palm, nibbling. She giggled, patting her nose.

"Time is of the essence, girl," King Saul said. "Come, quickly."

The king surprised her again by holding out his hand. She took it, and he tugged her up into his chariot beside him. Grabbing the reins, he slapped them over the horses' backs, and they jumped, trotting into the dark. Men jogged alongside them, with one moving ahead with lamps to light their path.

Sanura peered into the darkness, praying the horses would not fall into some great crack in the earth and send them all to their death.

When the horses climbed the side of a steep hill, Sanura's knuckles whitened as she grasped the edge of the chariot on its ascent. The king stepped down, offering his hand again. She took it, and as her feet touched down on soft grass, the dead beneath her stirred.

"Tell me his name, my king."

"Samuel."

"Your men must leave us," she said. "Only those whose ears the message is intended for may be present."

King Saul nodded and turned, barking orders at his men. When they had cleared the hill, and only Sanura and the king remained, she knelt, pressing her hands to the ground. Closing her eyes, she let the hum of lingering souls guide her magic until she found the one she sought. King Samuel had been great indeed and his lingering essence sang louder than those buried beside him. Tugging at the frayed remains of his soul, she pulled it loose from that eternal slumber.

King Samuel's soul stirred.

"Arise, Samuel, and speak with me." Her voice, nothing like the soft, tentative one reserved for men in high stations, was strong and clear. What she commanded would be done; the dead could not deny her.

The ground rumbled, and Sanura stood, dusting her knees. King Saul backed up as the earth trembled and shook, and soon, a bony hand broke free. It stretched and scraped at the dirt, joined by a second.

When he had pulled himself free from his resting place, King Samuel's empty sockets—set back in bleached bone—watched her far too keenly. A shiver rolled through her at his eerie vacant stare.

King Saul moved up behind her, letting her shield him from the creature who watched them both.

When Samuel spoke, bones popped, and his jaw moved unnaturally. "Why have you disturbed me?"

"Ask him your questions, my king," Sanura said, stepping aside.

King Saul moved forward, limbs trembling as he dropped to the ground, touching his head to the earth at the dead king's feet.

"I am in great distress," he began. "The Philistines fight against me, and my father has turned his back on our people. He no longer answers me, either by prophets or dreams. So, I have called on you to give me guidance."

Samuel's skeleton seemed to consider his question before saying, "Why do you consult me now that our father has become your enemy?"

A chill ran down Sanura's spine as she watched the two kings speaking. She could almost feel the empty eyes of Samuel on her, and in her chest, something tugged her toward him. Though she was no stranger to the magic that begged to be set free any time she confronted death, there was something different about this soul. Something *stronger.* She backed up, giving the men privacy to speak, and wandered to the horses grazing farther down the hill.

Even as she moved away, that tug became more insistent, but she ignored it, running a hand over the mare's muscular neck. The horse flicked her tail, ignoring Sanura as she munched, moving down the hill to a new patch of grass.

When the night had stretched long and the pre-dawn chill crept into Sanura's bones, King Saul found her. He was ashen-faced in the silvery moonlight. "Must we return him to his rest?"

Sanura shook her head. "I called him only for the night. When day breaks he will return to the dirt."

Finding the handle of his chariot, the king pulled himself up, seeming to forget she was there. One of his guards, the same one she'd noticed before with strong calves and stronger thighs, held out a hand to her.

"My lady," he said as he lifted her into the chariot.

She looked up, staring into the bluest eyes she'd ever beheld as he met her golden ones. Her gaze dropped, prepared for the fear or disgust she saw on so many men's faces when they glimpsed her strange eyes, but his grip tightened on her fingers, warm and reassuring. Meeting his gaze once more, something stirred in her chest. He wasn't looking away. He was staring intently.

FATED

As though he had never seen anything or anyone more perfect.

CHAPTER 2

Sanura

Sanura reached her family home just before the sun breached the horizon. Her stomach fluttered as the soldier who had helped her into the cart gripped her fingers tightly, ushering her to her door.

Watching him go, a pang of something she couldn't name burned in her chest.

When they were specks in the distance, she crept inside, careful not to wake her sleeping parents. She had yet to finish packing and would be expected to be up in less than an hour. Chores were the backbone of a strong society, her father always said, and even if she were leaving her family, perhaps forever, they would have to be finished before they began the long trek toward the sea.

Resigning herself to her fate, she moved to the corner of the room, stuffing her belongings into her bag.

The night had been long, and though she hadn't expected praise from a king, she thought he would at least offer a kind word. Instead, he had left her outside her home without a backward glance and disappeared into the night.

Her mind strayed to the golden-haired soldier, and her hand spasmed at the memory of his touch. When their fingers met, energy raced up her arm, igniting a pulsing warmth in her chest as heat simmered in his vibrant eyes.

Sanura laughed at her fanciful thoughts. He was a king's guard, and she was a peasant's daughter and wielder of dark magic. Anything she'd felt had surely been one-sided.

When her bag was packed, she left her home, tracing a worn path to the goat pen, where her two favorite creatures bleated when they saw her. Stopping at the gate, she lifted hay from its pile, dropping it into the corner of their pen, and patted the speckled nose of the first goat, even as the second nudged her arm for attention. She had wanted to name them when they were born, but her father scolded her, saying: *We do not name our food, Sanura.*

She scratched behind one's ear, whispering, "I would never eat you." Her goat bleated merrily, and she smiled, scratching him harder.

"You're good with animals," a deep voice said.

Sanura spun in the waning darkness, searching for the owner of that silky voice.

The king's soldier stepped out of the shadows, streaks of orange dawn light glinting off his golden locks.

"You scared me," she breathed, pressing a hand to her chest.

He stepped closer. "I didn't mean to."

Some invisible magnetism pulled her forward, dragging her toward him, and her feet moved. She was in front of him, staring up at a man who might have been carved from the sheerest stone walls for his impressive stature and broad shoulders. He was tall, bronzed, and devastatingly handsome.

"Does your king require my service?"

He shook his head. "He bade me bring compensation for your trouble."

She swallowed as the words rolled over her skin like a soft caress, so lost in the timbre of his voice that she'd almost missed the words. "Compensation?"

"Your father told me of your plans to travel to Athens," he explained. "I will escort you. Keep you safe."

Sanura backed up, inhaling sharply. She'd been impossibly close, improperly so, and her heart thrashed wildly in her chest. "I... That is... There is no need."

The soldier moved with her, closing the distance she had put between them, and caught her hand in his, holding it the way he had when he lifted her out of the chariot less than an hour before.

"I must. My king commands it."

Wrapped in his, Sanura's hand burned as she marveled at how soft the hands of a king's guard could be. But when he spoke again, all her focus returned to his face and the narrow space between them—growing narrower by the moment.

"Would you condemn me to death?"

"I... No. Never."

He smiled, and she held her breath, determined to burn that perfect image into her mind forever.

"Sanura, what is the meaning of this?"

Her father's sharp tone jolted through her, and she tore her hand from the soldier's, turning to face him. "Father. The king has sent..."

The guard stepped past her, tipping his head in a sign of respect toward her father. "I am Ba'al, sir. King Saul sent me to escort your daughter as payment for her service."

Sanura's father glanced between his daughter and the soldier bowed before him. No one ever tipped their head to him; he was of no importance in their village.

"Rise, Ba'al," her father said, standing a little taller. "I am honored by the king's blessing. Please, join us as we break fast before we depart."

Sanura's stomach flipped as Ba'al rose, following her father into their tiny home. Her cheeks flushed imagining what he must think of their dwelling after living in the king's palace.

Her mother met them at the door, dipping her head to their visitor, and ushered them to sit as she moved about the small space, bringing bread, water, oil, and spices. She set two apples on their table, and Sanura grimaced, knowing her mother had been saving them for her journey.

Ba'al said nothing, seeming right at home in their space. When they had finished their meal, her gaze snagged on the two apples still sitting on the table.

When Sanura had loaded her bag onto their cart, she walked behind it with Ba'al. The sun hung low in the sky by the time they reached port. Sanura raised a hand overhead, shielding her eyes as she gazed out at the expanse of blue stretching across the horizon. She hadn't truly considered what it would mean to be at sea for ten days. One full week. Now, staring into the distance, the vastness of the world stretched out before her, and she felt very small.

A warm hand found hers and squeezed. She glanced down at the tanned fingers that had touched hers so many times that day. Any time her father slipped away to haggle with some landowner or inspect goods to be traded, he was there, finding her fingers and wrapping them in his. Each time he touched her, a new round of butterflies erupted in her stomach.

"I don't want to go," she said. "I want to stay with you."

"Sanura." Ba'al released her hand, stepping back as her father turned to look at them. "I thought you understood. I'm coming with you."

CHAPTER 3

Sanura

Ten long days after Sanura left her home, stepping off the safety of dry land into the wild blue sea, something began to take shape on the horizon. Seagulls cried overhead, and her stomach settled for the first time in days.

Ba'al reached for her hand, squeezing it. Though he'd paid for their passage in labor, rowing with the other men, stacking crates, or seeing to any other task they gave him, he'd found her several times each day to take her hand in his.

It was a gentle reminder he hadn't left her to make this journey alone.

Though she was relieved to set foot on dry land after so many days, something in her chest twisted at the idea that her soldier would be returning to Israel while she would continue on to her new life.

"Sanura."

She glanced back, meeting his bright blue stare. "Yes, Ba'al?"

"You must make me a promise."

Her gaze darted back to the landmass approaching on the horizon. "Mmh-mm."

"Sanura." His fingers tightened on hers, and the urgency in his voice had her focusing on him. "The witches here are very superstitious. You cannot tell them about your magic."

Sanura's stomach hollowed out. Her mother had advised her to guard her secret closely from the day her gift had manifested. The king had come under cover of darkness, not wishing to be found out, but Ba'al was one of two soldiers who had heard their conversation. Was she wrong to trust him with this knowledge?

"Don't worry," he said, searching her face. "I would never tell a soul. But you can't trust anyone with your secret."

She swallowed. "I wouldn't. I don't."

"Good. Even if you think you can. Even if you find... a lover."

Her cheeks heated at his words. They were bold, uncouth words for a man to speak to anyone other than his wife. But she seemed far more affected by them than he had, and he was watching her, waiting for a response.

"I won't." She pulled her fingers from his grip, and her chest spasmed.

His gaze slid over her face, resting on her lips. He nodded, straightening and backed up as two passengers came to stand beside them, eyeing Ba'al strangely. He'd grown increasingly bolder with his touches as they neared Athens, and she thanked Athena no one had seen them together. If they had, she'd have been tossed overboard for her indecency without question. Of course, Ba'al wouldn't be questioned—he was a man.

Their captain shouted orders to the men, and Ba'al left her side to help as they jumped into the water and began wading toward the shore. When their boat was tied off, scraping mud just offshore, people began jumping out, holding their belongings overhead.

Sanura lifted her bag, preparing to step overboard, when strong arms wrapped around her waist, lifting her out of the boat. Her face was on fire as Ba'al set her down several feet closer to shore. Only her sandals and calves had gotten wet. She sloshed away from him, squeezing her eyes shut in hopes no one had seen his hands on her. Thankfully, everyone seemed too preoccupied with their belongings or their loved ones to notice his actions.

"Sanura. Sanura!" a voice called over the hustle and bustle of activity around her.

She searched the crowd, seeing a young man waving his arms overhead. She marched toward him, glancing back only once to see Ba'al talking with the boatman before she continued up the beach, meeting the man who'd called her name.

"Are you Sanura?"

"Yes," she said, bowing her head. "Uncle Antyamos?"

He chuckled, drawing her gaze up to his face. "Dionysus, no. I'd never be caught dead claiming to be that old bag. I'm Lysander, second son of House Gavras." He bowed low, making her giggle.

"Is that all you brought?" he asked, sliding her bag off her shoulder and slinging it over his arm. "Come on, everyone's dying to meet you. Cool eyes, by the way. I've never met anyone with eyes of gold before."

Sanura cast her gaze to the ground, squeezing her hands into fists. In a new land less than a moment and already she'd been careless. She knew better than to look another person in the eyes in full daylight.

"Hey, no worries. We have some strange people here. You'll see."

"Your speech is so... modern," she said, looking up through her lashes.

He laughed again. "You're in the big city now. You'll find a lot of the country customs were abandoned the moment people slapped sandals on modern stone." She smiled, looking up to meet his eyes again. "Come on. We don't want to be late," he continued. "Mother's temper is famous when anyone is late for supper."

Sanura glanced back again, searching the boat for Ba'al. She'd meant to say goodbye, to thank him, to see if he cared to stay in touch, but when she scanned the men loading new cargo onto the boat, she didn't see him anywhere. Her heart sank.

"Coming, Cuz?"

Sanura pulled a braid over her shoulder and tugged it as she trailed after Lysander.

"That's Cecropia, the Acropolis of Athens. It's where your uncle spends all his time," Lysander whispered, pointing up at a massive stone structure.

Her gaze followed the direction of his finger to the largest building she'd ever seen at the top of a tall, flat hill. It seemed to be the central focus of this vast, bustling city. They proceeded up a steep path, sliding to one side as carts pulled by mules passed them on the road. On the way, Lysander continued pointing out landmarks, temples, and the mountains rimming the horizon.

Sanura's feet ached when they reached the peak of a tall hill and stopped outside another architectural wonder.

"What building is this?" she breathed, staring up at the impressive stone facade.

"This is home."

She gaped, taking in the expansive walls before her, and blew out a long breath as she counted not two rows of windows but three. Never in her wildest dreams had Sanura imagined she would step inside a home with three floors.

"Who's your friend?"

Sanura started as she realized another man had stepped up beside them.

"This is my cousin, Sanura," Lysander said. "She's here from Endor. Come to be part of Helena's little coven." Lysander rolled his eyes but gave her a wide smile, letting her know he was only joking.

A genuine smile crept over her face at his teasing tone.

"Hey," the stranger said. "I'm Menelaos, Lysander's friend."

"I thought you were *my* friend," an elegant voice called as a third man stepped through the arched doors of Lysander's home. He was classically handsome, dripping with wealth, and not at all Sanura's type.

She dipped her head, bowing low to the Eupatridae man, knowing at once he must be of some high-born house.

"No need for that, girl," he said, stopping before her. "I'm Erasmos, Helena's intended. That nearly makes us family."

Sanura lifted her head and didn't miss the grimace Erasmos tried to hide behind all that class before he schooled his features into one of blank passivity that would have made her mother proud. Thinking of Shalim made her heart twist. It had been ten days since she'd seen her mother—the longest they'd been apart in her life.

"This is Sanura," Lysander said, filling in the awkward silence.

A pang of homesickness hit her, and she bit the inside of her cheek, blinking back tears. She would not cry in front of these strangers. She said it in her mind, repeating the words until her vision cleared. When she looked up, all three men were staring at her strangely. Had she done something? Shown some bit of her gift? The death dwelling in this foreign land had been overwhelming when they began their trek, but as they moved outside the city, it had abated, and she could almost ignore death's pull.

"Cousin!" a feminine voice trilled, making Sanura jump. A gorgeous girl with ringlets spun from gold cascading down her back raced through the courtyard, clasping Sanura's hands tightly. She moved as if on air, golden skin wrapped in the lightest fabric Sanura had ever seen, dyed in a soft saffron hue. "I've dreamed of this day!"

15

Sanura watched her full pink lips move as she spoke, caught in some trance.

"It will be so delightful to have a reprieve from all these men," she was saying, and Sanura registered some of her words.

"You must be Helena."

CHAPTER 4

Sanura

Helena laughed as Sanura swayed on her feet, leaning into her cousin's embrace.

"Whoa," Lysander said, stepping forward. "Come on, Helena, cut it out."

When her cousin released her, Sanura's mind cleared, and she stumbled backward. "You're a siren!"

Helena's lips parted, forming an o. "I thought you were a powerful witch. That's what father said. I didn't think I'd have to keep my gifts in check with you. I see that's not the case." Her words were haughty, and a little disappointed, and Sanura's cheeks flamed.

"Dionysus, Helena. Stop showing off," Lysander scolded her. "Everyone knows you're the best. You don't have to put her in her place before she even sets foot through the door."

Helena's slender golden brow rose, her lips puckering as she prepared to give her brother a piece of her mind.

"Enough, children. Let us be gracious hosts to our new guest who's traveled far."

The siblings slid apart as a tall, graceful woman, draped in robes of white with gold rope tied in an intricate pattern along her torso and over her shoulders, stepped between them, and held out her hand.

Sanura bowed, kissing the woman's prominent golden ring.

"You must be Sanura," she said, not inviting Sanura to rise.

Sanura kept her head bowed as she nodded. "Father bade me bring fond wishes."

"Rise, Sanura," she said, laughing.

Sanura lifted her head, meeting the woman's intense stare.

"I'm Leontia, matron of this house. You may address me as such."

Sanura dipped her head again.

"Helena, show Sanura to her room and prepare her for supper."

Lysander handed Sanura her bag, and she followed Helena through an arched doorway leading into an open courtyard. At its center, stone carved into a school of fish leaped from a fountain, clear water spouting from their mouths into a shallow pool. Sanura's mouth dropped open as she marveled at the intricate designs on each fish, more beautiful than any stonework she'd seen. Even her village's grand bust of their king paled in comparison.

They passed several arched doors to her left and right, and Sanura peeked in, seeing house staff bustling quickly around the large spaces. They passed a room with a massive low table at its center and cushions set around it as they continued toward the rear of the house.

Helena moved quickly up a staircase at the back of the courtyard, leading the way down a covered hall with several doors. She stopped at the entrance to a room with one small window and a bed along the wall.

"This room only has one bed," Sanura said in confusion.

Helena covered her mouth, laughing softly. "We do not share rooms here, Cousin."

Sanura crinkled her nose. She studied her cousin, searching for a lie in her words. Now that Helena had released her from her siren spell, Sanura saw that while Helena was comely, her fine clothing and jewelry were her most appealing attributes. She stepped into the room, stopping beside the bed. The room she shared with her mother and father was smaller than this one by half and made up most of their dwelling. Never had she imagined she would find herself in such a fine home.

Setting her bag down, she spied a dark carved chest at the end of the bed. "It's beautiful," she whispered, running a hand over polished wood.

"Come on, you can borrow something of mine until we get you a few garments of your own." Helena moved into the hall. "Women are on this side of the house, and men are on that side." She pointed to a row of doors farther down the hall. "Don't get caught on their side, or Father will tan your hide."

Sanura nodded, following Helena into the room across from hers. Helena slid her own dark chest open, pulling out swaths of silky fabric in shades of gold, white, lavender, and saffron, laying them out on her bed. She looked up, giving Sanura a quizzical eye before digging to the bottom of the chest and pulling out cobalt fabric.

"I think this would suit your dark hair." She held it up, pulling one of Sanura's braids over her shoulder. "And we must fix this."

When Sanura was dressed in her cousin's fine silk, her hair unbound and brushed, a slender golden band was nestled into her wavy locks, resting just above both ears. Helena expertly rolled all the hair around her face through the band so only small strands framed her face, leaving most of her long hair running down her back. Helena held out her mirror, and Sanura took it, admiring her transformation. She turned her head from side to side, loving the glint of gold sparkling below her ears as it held her thick hair in place. It was functional yet appealing.

Helena lifted a pot and small paintbrush from her table in the room's corner. She dipped her brush into the pot and lifted it to Sanura's face.

"What's that?" Sanura asked, ducking out of her cousin's reach.

"It enhances your eyes." Helena stretched her brush out.

Sanura took another step back. "No. Please. I do not want to draw attention to my eyes."

Helena set her pot down, resting the brush against the lip of the jar. "You have beautiful eyes. Unique. Some young man will be tempted by them, I'm sure."

Sanura's cheeks burned, her mind wandering to Ba'al. He had not been afraid of her eyes. He'd met them boldly more than once. Her heart sank, knowing she would likely never see him again. "Are you not afraid of their odd color?"

"Why ever would I be?" Helena replied. "They're your most striking attribute, apart from your glossy crimson hair. You'll find a husband in no time."

Sanura's stomach flipped. She was old for a maiden, she knew. All the girls in her village had been married several years younger, but her strangeness had always kept the village men at bay. She shook her head. "I prefer to leave my skin untouched."

Helena shrugged. "Let's go down to supper, then. Mother will be angry if we stall much longer."

They sat around a large rectangular stone table, men on one side, women on the other, as house staff moved around them, bringing grape leaves, fruits, cured meat, and ale. It was a feast for a king, but the others around the table hardly touched their food.

Sanura ate ravenously, stuffing everything that touched her plate into her mouth. She hadn't eaten meat in longer than she could remember, and her mother only made grape leaves on special occasions.

"Are you settled in your room, Sanura?" Leontia lifted her cup to her lips, watching Sanura over the rim.

She looked up, swallowing her mouth full of food, but before she could answer, Helena spoke up. "She brought nothing with her, and her shawl is little better than a rag," she said. "We must take her to market, Mother."

Leontia arched a brow at her daughter but nodded. "I suppose you're right. We can't have our cousin going about town in peasant garb."

"I'll take her," Lysander said, smiling shyly.

"No," Leontia said. "Erasmos, take your betrothed and buy her something nice, won't you? You and Helena can show Sanura our city after supper."

Erasmos tipped his head to his mother-in-law-to-be and gave Helena a subtle grin.

Leontia's too-sharp gaze missed nothing, and she said, "And take Aesop."

"Mother, no," Helena groaned.

The youngest person at the table perked up at this, and Sanura could only assume he was Aesop.

"You'll take your brother, or you will not go."

Helena lifted her cup to her lips, drinking deeply, and her bronzed cheeks darkened. She stood, not waiting to be dismissed, and stormed from the room.

"You'll need to get your bride under control, Erasmos, if you hope to seat yourself beside her father in the Senate."

He frowned, stood, and bowed to Leontia.

Sanura watched the matron under her lashes, awed by the woman who seemed to manage her home quite deftly in her husband's absence. Sanura had never met a woman who gave orders to men or was paid such respect. She had yet to meet her uncle. He was important, she knew, one of the wealthiest landowners in Athens, and that wealth gave him power. Did it also extend to his wife?

The boy across from her, Aesop, stood. "Mother, may I go?"

She gave her youngest child an indulgent smile. "Yes, my darling. Look after your cousin, and for the love of Athena, keep an eye on your sister."

CHAPTER 5

Sanura

S anura looked up, watching as Erasmos slid a gold cuff up the inside of Helena's arm, letting his fingers graze the bare skin along the side of her breast. Her cheeks darkened as she glanced around, but no one seemed to be paying them any attention.

Sanura felt a tug at her gown and spun around to find Aesop behind her, holding out a honey cake.

"Is this for me?" she asked, smiling.

He nodded and placed it in her waiting palm.

She laughed, biting into her gift, delighting in the sweetness paired with flaky breading and crunchy almonds. Her eyes closed as she savored its flavor. She'd had baklava only once when a traveling merchant offered it to her father and he shared a bite with her. When she opened her eyes, Aesop had disappeared again, and she licked her fingers, continuing her perusal of the market.

In her village, market days happened only once a week. On those days, traders from neighboring villages scraped together any spare goods they had to trade with one another. Here, in the bustling city of Athens, there were rows upon rows of goods to buy if one had the coin to spend.

Helena's tinkling laugh caught her ear, and she looked up in time to spy Erasmos pulling her indecently close. Aesop appeared and wedged himself between his sister and her betrothed. Helena rolled her eyes but let Aesop drag her away from Erasmos to a stand selling small carved boxes. Erasmos glared after them,

22

and Sanura wondered momentarily if the boy was in danger. She'd seen that look in men's eyes before—nothing good ever followed.

Something tugged at her gown again, and she looked down in confusion. A child, streaked in dirt, covered only in rags, stared up at her with large, pleading eyes.

She knelt and asked, "Are you hungry?" The child nodded, eyes misting. "Don't worry, child. We will find you something to eat."

Sanura took the child's dirty hand, and they moved through the market. She scanned a fruit vendor's counter, smiling when she spied a small honey cake like the one Aesop had brought her moments before. "May I have one of these?" she asked the vendor.

"That'll be an iron."

"An iron?" Sanura nearly choked her response. In her village, an iron would have bought five loaves of bread. Could the small cake truly be so expensive?

"We'll take two," a deep voice said, making her spin.

She gasped as Ba'al stepped up behind her, handing two coins to the vendor. He took them, handing over two cakes. Ba'al offered one to the child, who squealed in delight, and the other to her.

"Ba'al! I thought you left."

His bright, azure eyes twinkled in amusement. "Did you think I would leave you among the wolves?"

Sanura's heart raced as he stepped closer, close enough for her to make out the starburst pattern rimming his irises as his sweet breath kissed her face. She had leaned in without realizing it and quickly backed up, swaying on her feet. He caught her arm, steadying her, and heat radiated up her arm.

"I... I don't understand. Your King needs you," she said.

"I couldn't leave. Not without knowing you were safe."

She swallowed, feeling that invisible pull drag her forward once more. Something solid slammed into her hip, and she stumbled back as Aesop wrapped his arms around her legs.

"Aesop, what are you doing?" Sanura laughed, and he spun her around, making the world spin even after she'd stopped. "Aesop, this is..." she turned in a circle, but Ba'al was go"Aesop, did you see a man?" Sanura asked. "He was standing beside me."

"I saw him. He's a bad man. I rescued you from him." He beamed up at her, but she frowned.

"No, Aesop. He's my friend from back home."

"I don't think you should talk to him anymore."

Sanura's brows crinkled. "Do you know him?"

"No. But I know what he is."

"There you are, Cousin!" Helena called out. "I've been looking everywhere. Mother sent us to buy you clothes. What are you doing playing with Aesop?" Helena's cheeks were stained a deep bronze, and she looked as though she had run to meet them.

Sanura looked past Helena and Aesop, scanning the crowd for a man with golden hair and the most beautiful eyes she'd ever seen. But he was gone.

When they returned from the market, Helena's arms were full of new fabrics, hairpins, headbands, and cuffs, and Aesop carried desserts for his mother and brother. Erasmos trailed silently behind them. Sanura hadn't missed the odd looks he gave Helena or how she avoided meeting his eyes.

Lysander greeted them at the door, taking Sanura's new garments from her and offering to take them upstairs.

"Mother would never allow it, Lysander," Helena said with a laugh. "But since you're being useful, you can take mine too." She piled her new purchases in his arms and moved past him into the kitchens.

Erasmos stalked after Helena, and Sanura scurried past the door as his raised voice carried through the walls.

"How did you like our market?" Lysander asked, adjusting his hold on their garments.

"Let me take some of those," Sanura said, grabbing a handful of fabric. "It was enormous. I don't think I've ever seen so many vendors in my life."

Lysander gave her a lopsided grin. "That was nothing. Wait until harvest day. And after a day of shopping, we feast and dance all night."

"It sounds—" Sanura's words were abruptly cut off as Erasmos stormed from the kitchens and tore the fabric from her arms.

"You will have nothing else from me, spoiled brat!" His eyes were red-rimmed, burning with murderous intent as Helena slid to a stop before him, saying nothing. He reached for the cuff wrapped around Sanura's arm, but Lysander dropped the things in his hands and caught Erasmos's biceps first.

Erasmos turned his violent gaze on Lysander, and behind him, water in the fountain began to swirl, shooting into the air.

Sanura stumbled back, throwing her hands up to shield herself as a wave rushed them.

Lysander dropped his hold on Erasmos, throwing his arms up, and the oncoming water battered against an invisible shield, sliding harmlessly away. He dropped his shield and cupped both hands as an immense ball of flame formed in his palms.

Erasmos cupped his own hands, forming purple flame.

Helena ducked behind Lysander, grabbed Sanura's arm, and tugged her up the stairs. "Come on, Cousin, we don't want to get in the middle of their fight."

"What? What's happening?" Sanura stumbled behind Helena as she was dragged up the stairs.

When they reached the second floor, Helena stopped and leaned over the railing. Sanura moved on shaky legs to stand beside her. Her mouth fell open as Lysander and Erasmos circled one another, firing ball after ball of flame only to block it and send another back.

Sanura's voice shook as she said, "they'll kill each other."

"Erasmos would deserve it," Helena said viciously.

Sanura swiveled her gaze to her cousin, who seemed too caught up in their fight to notice her horrified stare.

Erasmos lunged forward, knocking Lysander to the ground, and Sanura's focus returned to their fight. Erasmos pressed both hands against his chest, and Sanura gasped as Lysander seemed to be sucked into the ground before them.

"Enough," Leontia's voice called, and Erasmos stopped, holding up his hands.

Lysander flew up on some unnatural wind, gasping for breath and dusting dirt and debris from his clothes. He charged forward, but Leontia held up a hand, and he froze midstep.

"Erasmos, take your leave," Leontia said.

He spun on his heel, giving none of them a second glance.

Sanura raced back down the stairs, reaching Lysander's side, panting. She raised a shaking hand to his face, wiping dirt from his cheek.

25

"He will be fine, child." Leontia touched her son's other cheek, and some of the rage in his eyes banked. To her son, she said, "Go clean yourself up and get your temper under control."

Sanura let her hand fall, watching him storm away.

Leontia gave her a kind smile. "You'll forgive the men in this house. Too much pent-up energy." Sanura's tongue was thick in her mouth, but Leontia didn't wait for her reply as she turned to her daughter. "Come down here, Helena, and explain yourself."

Sanura backed away, taking the matron's words as dismissal. Picking up their discarded garments, her pulse raced as she tried to make sense of everything she had just witnessed. Her heart sank as she lifted scorched fabrics and ran their charred, blackened remains between her fingers.

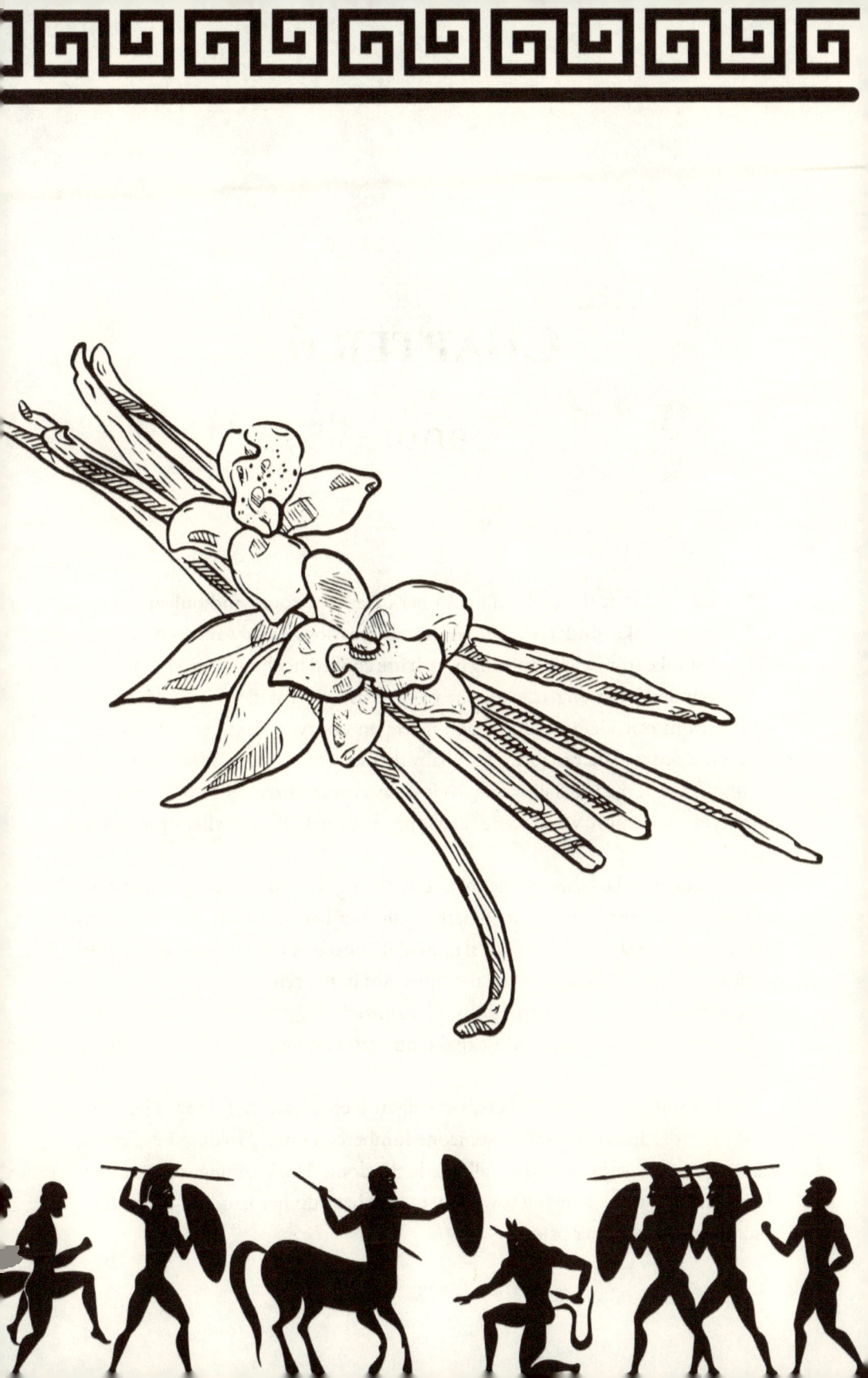

CHAPTER 6

Sanura

Sanura stared at the dark ceiling in her cavernous room and pulled her soft cotton blanket under her chin. At home, the room had always been suffocating, and smoke from a low-burning hearth fire choked her lungs, even in summer.

Surrounded by strangers, the ache of her family's distance set in. In Endor, sounds from outside drifted through her open doorway, and her father's light snores melded together to form the lullaby that sang her to sleep. Here, every light creak and scrape made her jump; she'd closed her eyes a dozen times, only to spring them wide once more when some small sound echoed off the walls of the Gavras home.

Silvery light spilled through her window, casting the room in shadows, and she imagined more than once that something sinister had slid over the floorboards toward her. She shot up as a door slammed downstairs. Garbled words followed by heavy footfall filtered up from the courtyard in the center of the home.

"Get back, woman," a man's deep voice slurred.

Softer words Sanura couldn't make out replied, and a loud crack echoed through the courtyard.

Sanura slid out of bed and crept on silent feet toward her door. The stairs creaked under heavy footfall as someone lumbered closer. Holding her breath, Sanura pressed her back to the wall beside the door. The shuffling stopped. Her door creaked open, swinging toward her—she held up her hands as it slammed against the backs of her palms.

"Where is she?"

"She feared sleeping alone, my love. She is sharing the room with Helena tonight."

"Wake'er up. I want to meet my sister's bastard."

"The girl has traveled a great distance, husband. Could we not allow her to rest this night, and she will present herself in the morning?"

Sanura exhaled a slow breath, squinting her eyes between the crack in the door. She held in a gasp as a man, nearly wider than he was tall, pulled his meaty hand back to strike his wife. She stepped sideways, preparing to speak and intervene, when Leontia ran the pad of her finger down her husband's cheek.

"Sleep, my love."

Sanura blinked several times, trying desperately to hold herself up even as she felt her body sliding down the wall.

Sanura woke with a start, finding herself in her new bed in her new home. A dream. It had been a dream. She sighed, tossing back her covers, and moved to the trunk at the end of her bed. She frowned, remembering her new garments had been burned to ash the night before.

A knock at her door had her looking up, and as it swung wide, the most intense sense of déjà vu hit her. Instead of the man from her dream, though, Helena stepped through.

"Morning, sleepyhead." She breezed into the room, decked in jewels and a powder white fabric that didn't cover nearly enough of her ample chest. "I wanted to say I'm sorry about last night. Erasmos has the most vile temper, and he's dreadfully jealous."

She sat on Sanura's crumpled blankets, smoothing white fabric over her knee. A light dusting of gold body powder shimmered in the morning light as she stared down at her hands. She looked up, meeting Sanura's gaze.

"The thing is, I have a secret."

Sanura came to sit beside her cousin, laying a hand over Helena's gold-dusted fingers. "Keep your secrets, Cousin. The affairs of you and your betrothed are not mine to know."

Wetness glistened at the corner of Helena's golden lashes as she met her cousin's eyes. "I will marry him. Father has commanded it, and I would never disobey him. And you must admit he's very nice to look at. If you can believe it, his family is richer than ours, but..."

Sanura released her cousin's hand, and Helena bit her lip, twisting the fabric between her fingers. Gold sparkled against the sheets as a tear spilled down Helena's cheek.

"I love someone else."

Sanura held her breath, wishing her cousin could take the words back. Wishing she could unhear them. Her whole life had been one secret after another, lies built on top of lies. The burden of them weighed heavily on her. She had no strength to carry other people's burdens on top of her own.

"His name is Aniel."

Sanura stood, pacing away from her cousin. "Please. Share no more with me."

Helena's tear-stained cheeks reddened, and she stood, her face twisting into something dark. She crossed the room, stopping in front of Sanura. "I was so excited when I knew you were coming. So looking forward to another woman in the house. Besides Mother." Her gaze shuddered. "But I see we aren't to be close friends."

Sanura opened her mouth, but Helena stormed from the room, bumping Leontia's shoulder as she fled.

Leontia gave her daughter a disapproving glance before returning her gaze to Sanura. "How did you sleep, child?"

Sanura searched the matron's face, noting the slightest hint of yellow along her cheekbone. The late night arrival of her uncle and the fight she'd witnessed... could it have been real? She shook her head. If she'd remembered correctly, Leontia would have a newly darkening bruise on her cheek, not one that looked to be faded and several days old.

"Well. Thank you, Matron."

Leontia's gaze roved over Sanura's sleep gown. "You must return to the market to replace the garments destroyed last night." She moved into the room, holding out her hands. "Come, you may borrow something of mine today."

CHAPTER 7

Sanura

"We must make a good impression on your new coven. Much will be determined in their first interaction with you."

Sanura nodded as she trailed Leontia through the busy market. By day, it was transformed. Where low torchlight and the soft glimmer of moonlight hid the city's filth and decay, the harsh morning sun cast Athens in a different light. Beggars squatted in piss and waste-filled corners, children whose ribs cut through thin fabric stared vacantly at nothing, and vendors cast wary gazes at the crowd, hands hovering over glinting objects at their waists.

"Come, child. We must return before my husband wakes."

Sanura rushed past a dangerous-looking group with dark eyes who watched closely as Leontia withdrew a small purse from her hip. She nearly tripped over too-long fabric as she caught up to the matron and stopped beside a vendor selling fabrics in rich shades of every color. Leontia reached for tan, common among unmarried women, but Sanura moved around her, running her fingers over a swath of deep green fabric.

"May I choose my colors, Matron?"

Leontia raised a dark brow, but her lips split in that same indulgent smile she had shared with Aesop. "Of course. Green is a bold and beautiful color. The coven will respect you all the more for wearing it."

Sanura's heart thrummed in her chest. Meeting and being accepted by her new coven was the sole reason for coming to Athens. A rejection would mean a swift

31

departure, and Sanura needed to stay; even a fraction of the power she had already witnessed would change the fate of their village. If they could learn to mold earth, channel water, and call fire, they would see their town fed for a year on the crops they could grow and harvest. It would raise her father's station and change her position. Everything must go right.

Sanura lifted the fabric, running it between her fingers.

"Mother!" Sanura looked up as Lysander reached them, stopping beside her. "Hey, Sanura. I'm really sorry about last night."

Sanura's cheeks burned as she looked away from Lysander. He was staring at her a little too earnestly for her liking, and her stomach flipped as his dark eyes bored into her.

"It's okay."

"Lysander will buy your new things," Leontia said. "Punishment for his behavior."

Lysander grinned, stretching a hand out to run it over the green fabric on the counter. His fingers brushed hers, and she tugged her hand back.

"Be quick, Lysander. Your father expects a formal introduction at the morning meal, and we will go from there to the temple to meet Kassandra and the others." Leontia turned her gaze on Sanura. "Will you be alright with Lysander while I run a quick errand?"

Sanura nodded, her stomach flipping again, though she wasn't entirely sure why.

Aesop skidded to a halt beside them, and Lysander's grin dropped. "Aesop, why are you here?"

"Helena sent me to remind you that you burned her things, too."

Lysander's full lips turned down as he glared at his sibling. "Tell Helena—"

"Lysander. You owe your sister as well," Leontia called over her shoulder as she disappeared into the crowd.

"Lysander!"

The group looked up as Lysander's friend from the day before joined them.

"Menelaos, what brings you to market this morning?"

"Father sent me to collect from the vendors." He gave Lysander a knowing look as Sanura stared between them in confusion.

"Menelaos's father is our city's tax collector," Lysander explained. "One of them."

Menelaos nodded.

"What is a tax?" Sanura asked, forehead wrinkling.

"It's the money owed to sell goods here," Menelaos said. "Vendors must pay it to offer their wares to the people of Athens."

Sanura reached for one of her ringlets, tugging it as she gave Menelaos another confused stare. It made little sense to her, but a glance at the sun rising ever higher into the sky had her stomach churning. "Perhaps you will explain it to me later. I'm afraid I have no time today."

"I can explain better than he can. I'll tell you after supper," Lysander said, giving her a wink.

Menelaos rolled his eyes, patting his friend on the back. "Come find me if you want a real lesson in mathematics. Lysander's never had to add sums before. He hands over coin, and the vendors swindle him every time."

Aesop giggled, and Lysander scowled.

"I'm sorry, Cousin, could we hurry?" Sanura asked. "I do not want to keep your father waiting."

Lysander sobered at her words and, as Menelaos had predicted, handed over far too much coin for her fabric. They moved from stand to stand, Sanura tugging her curls harder each time he presented a new object and its price. Still, Lysander dug into his seemingly bottomless purse. As his arms grew fuller, a rumble started at her midsection, and she held a hand over her belly to cover the sound.

"Hungry?"

She nodded.

"Let's get something to eat."

"Father would be furious!" Aesop interjected, and something in Lysander's bright gaze darkened.

"You're right, little Sop. Let's get going before he wakes in one of his moods."

Sanura watched her shadow stretch across the packed earth and looked up. "Does he truly sleep so late?"

Aesop bobbed his head vigorously. "He never wakes before mid-day. And the later he wakes, the worse it is for the rest of us."

An image flashed through Sanura's mind: A meaty hand pulled back, prepared to strike. She blinked it away.

"Come, Sanura, Aesop is right," Lysander said. "We need to get back before he wakes."

Sanura raced after the two Gavras brothers, her stomach flipping for an entirely new reason. What sort of man was she sharing a roof with?

As she moved swiftly through the market, bright golden hair reflected the sun, standing nearly a head above the surrounding men. Sanura's breath caught, and she knew before he ever turned who it would be.

CHAPTER 8

Sanura

S anura met Leontia at the entrance to the courtyard and exhaled sharply when Leontia gave them all a nod. He had not yet awoken. She raced to her room, dumping her new clothes on her bed before she left, moving silently down the hall. She'd wanted nothing more than to stop and speak with Ba'al, to ask how she could contact him again, but as she rushed by, he had disappeared among the men. He had been a mirage; her mind playing tricks on her.

It seemed her mind was becoming entirely unreliable in this new place; that frightened her more than she dared admit.

At the market, a tug had started in her chest, and it had only grown more insistent. Though that often meant the dead were calling her, begging to be awoken, on rare occasions, that feeling was one of foreboding, a warning that death was coming for the people of their city.

Sanura stopped outside Helena's door and raised her arm to knock, but lowered voices caught her ear. She pressed her cheek to the door, listening. A man's voice spoke, startling her. She backed up as the door swung open, and Helena filled the frame, eyes narrowed to slits.

"Eavesdropping, Cousin?"

Sanura's gaze darted to the outline of a tall, broad-shouldered silhouette just before it vanished. She rubbed her eyes, taking another step back.

"I... I was only... bringing you your new clothes."

She thrust out her hands, and Helena's face softened. She peered into the hall behind Sanura, grabbed her wrist, and tugged her into the room.

"Get in here," she hissed, closing the door behind her. Helena whirled, taking her garments from Sanura and throwing them on her bed before spinning to face her cousin again. "I don't know what you think you saw, but—"

"I saw nothing."

Helena crossed her arms over her chest, raising a brow in a gesture very much like her mother's.

Sanura held up her hands. "Truly. I do not wish to interfere in your life. I meant what I said before. Your secrets are your own."

Helena's brow lowered, but her arms remained tucked over her chest. "Our Pythia is my closest friend, you know. What she sees will determine your fate with the coven." She stalked closer. "I will ensure she gives you a favorable reading if you swear never to share anything you've seen."

Sanura touched Helena's arm. "Cousin, you mistake me," she said. "I have my own secrets, too many to possibly hold any of yours. Please keep them and know I would never betray you."

Helena's lips twitched up, her arms loosening. "What secrets? Tell me." Her excitement radiated through the room, sending the objects on her table rattling in agitation.

Sanura glanced around nervously. "Are you doing that?"

Helena's mouth flattened, and the objects around her stilled. She swung her arms freely as she moved to her table and picked up her brush. "Honestly, Cousin. I thought you were supposed to be powerful. What gifts do you actually have?"

Sanura swallowed. She'd known this test was coming, had prepared for it. She raised her hands, angling them toward the brush in Helena's grip, and curled her fist. At her command, the wood curled and twisted, bending until the handle spiraled. She curled two fingers toward her palms, and the wood darkened to a deep auburn.

Helena stared down at the object, lips parting. When nothing else happened, she glanced up. "Huh. That's a neat trick, I guess." Striding forward, she pressed the newly shaped brush into Sanura's chest. "Keep it. I'll get a new one."

She slipped out the door as Sanura turned slowly, wiping a sweaty palm down her leg.

In the same room they'd met for dinner the night before, Sanura sat beside Helena. She glanced at the empty space between Lysander and Aesop, then back to Leontia. Leontia had changed into a peplos far more elegant than the one she'd worn to market. By comparison, Sanura's new green robes were plain, even with the beautiful new scarab broach Lysander had insisted he buy her.

Helena was wearing the same white garb from that morning, but her arms each held three golden bands flecked with blue gems. In her hair, a golden circlet sparkled with matching blue stones. Her eyes were heavily lined, making her seem even more shrouded in secrets than before.

Leontia's arms were similarly banded, and two delicate golden cuffs circled her upper earlobes as well. On her head, a silver circlet held ruby and amethyst gems, nearly twice the size of Helena's.

Sanura glanced down at her own bare arms and wondered if she should have accepted one of the bands Lysander had offered to buy. At the time, they seemed extravagant—now she worried she would make a bad impression on their new coven.

An oppressive feeling settled over the room as all sound around her ceased. Sanura glanced up and swallowed. The man from her dream blocked the light as he filled the doorframe. Red bleary eyes scanned the room, settling on her. Her throat went dry as dark brows dipped low on his thick forehead.

"Father, let me intro—" Lysander's words died as his father's glare swiveled to him. He sat, cowed by a single look.

The blood drained from Sanura's face as his gaze returned to her.

"So." He stepped through the door, heavy steps bringing her dream back with sickening clarity. Not a dream. It was real. Sanura's gaze darted to Leontia, who seemed to know what she was thinking as she shook her head. "This is my sister's bastard."

"My love, please join us," Leontia said. "We have brought in eggs fresh from the coupe."

Antyamos Gavras ignored his wife, marching toward Sanura.

She slid back, rose, and dipped her head low, pressing her lips against his ruddy fingers, grazing coarse hairs along his knuckle. She shuddered but kept her head bowed, lips touching lightly against his skin as she awaited his next words. A light sweat broke out along her brow, and her knees trembled as they remained in that position longer than she'd ever been forced to bear it. The room remained deathly silent.

A deep bellow of laughter started in the gut directly at her eye level. "There now, a child with manners." Antyamos tore his fingers from her grip and backed up. Sanura's knees shook, but her head remained bowed, waiting for his word; his laugh continued as he backed away and, finally, left the room.

CHAPTER 9

Sanura

"Well, you survived your first encounter with Father."

"Lysander Gavras. Watch your tongue." Leontia's mouth was pressed into a tight line as she leveled a look on her son that might have sent others running. Lysander ducked his head as Sanura returned to her seat beside Helena, and her cousin squeezed her arm. That one comforting touch told her more than she ever wanted to know about the cruelty she'd endured.

Sanura hadn't been singled out. Every person at this table knew his callousness.

Sanura ran a sweaty palm down her jade robes, trailing Helena through sandstone pillars, staring up at ceilings that seemed to stretch into the Heavens. Never in all her seventeen years had she expected to find such a wonder on Earth. Her silent, bare feet touched cool stone as she moved through row after row of sculptures. Unlike the carvings and reliefs she had seen around Athens, each sculpture bore its own unique features. Erupting from their shoulders, beautiful feathered wings tapered to points as they reached the floor.

Sanura stopped before one statue, mesmerized by his sharp jawline and grand stature. His wings dragged along the floor, more stately than all the others. Across from him was a female angel—the first she'd seen in the long line of sculptures.

Helena stopped beside her. "He's magnificent, isn't he? Mother says he posed for it to ensure no detail was incorrect."

Sanura's mouth fell open. "This man lives in Athens? I hadn't imagined such a man existed in all the world."

Helena covered her smile with her hand. "He's not a man. Did you miss the wings?"

Sanura twisted to stare at her cousin. "Do you jest?"

"Come on. First, the reading. Then we'll share our secrets."

Sanura gazed up at the sculpture, taking in the angelic creature. Although he was undoubtedly the most beautiful man she had ever seen, sadness clung to him. His wings curved ever so slightly, and his gaze was downcast, unlike the others, who stared boldly ahead. Despite his looks, she couldn't help but compare him to her soldier. Where this sculpture was all darkness and despair, Ba'al was radiant light—a perfect contrast. Had they stood beside each other, it would have been difficult to choose which was more beautiful.

Leontia pressed several rough stones on the wall in an intricate pattern, and the floor rumbled as marble fell away, revealing a stairwell leading below the temple. She lifted a hand, her fingers lighting in a scarlet hue as she descended. Helena followed, and when she lifted her hand, her flame was a shade of soft morning sunlight. Sanura came last, something bitter twisting in her gut as she watched them cast their light so effortlessly.

At the bottom of the long, winding stairs, Leontia touched her fingers to the wall. Her flame chased an invisible track and illuminated the space in crimson light.

Sanura gasped as she surveyed the cavernous room filled with shallow pools of dark liquid on either side of a stone path. This far below the Earth, the room was naturally cool, and the moisture coating every surface coalesced in dewy droplets that fell in a patter of light rain. Her gaze trailed over an intricately carved relief spanning the room that seemed to tell a story of some great battle.

Humming at the far end of the room snagged Sanura's attention, and her gaze landed on a large circular bath draped in steam. Through the fog, lithe shapes reclined, dipping below the surface, and moved to the rhythm of their song. As she drew near, she was caught in their melody and the swirl of intertwined limbs. Three nude forms—locked in a tangle of caresses—moved to some unheard beat. The buzz of their chant tugged her forward, beckoning her to join, to touch.

She reached the edge of the pool and ran a hand over her shoulder, sliding the fabric of her tunic down. Her palm rubbed against heated skin and over her peaked nipple. A throbbing ache began low in her belly and radiated to the apex of her thighs. She slid her hand lower.

Cold fingers wrapped around her rogue hand, jarring her back to the present. Hazel eyes squinted, creasing at the edges as Leontia tipped her head back and cackled. "Athena take you, child. You have not been prepared."

Sanura wrenched her hand free and tugged soft green fabric up over her rapidly cooling skin. The fog in her mind cleared, giving her a full view of the large bathing pool and the dozen or so naked women lounging in it.

"Dianna!" someone called, and several women glided forward to greet them.

Sanura's cheeks burned, but in the low light, she desperately hoped no one noticed. Prayed no one had seen her touching herself in front of everyone. Helena's cruel smirk told her they had. And her face flushed.

"Aphrodite," a woman with dark curls and tanned skin called as she waded forward. She stood, showing off her shapely form. Her breasts hung heavy over a belly full with child. She emerged from the pool, embracing Helena.

"Why does she call you Aphrodite?"

Helena released her friend, winking at Sanura. "Coven secrets." She mimed sealing her lips and turned away from Sanura.

Helena's friend dressed quickly, followed by the other women in the pool, and soon, fifteen women stood around them, eyeing Sanura.

She clasped her fingers behind her back, straightening her shoulders as she worked to meet each of their eyes. Her mother's words came to mind: *You are every bit as powerful as they are, my brave girl. Show no weakness, but share none of your secrets.*

The pregnant woman stepped forward. "Welcome, Sanura, to Dina's Coven," she said. "Dianna has spoken to us of your many qualities. We hope she spoke true."

Sanura dipped her chin. "I hope to prove myself worthy, Pythia."

The coven's Pythia lowered her head before she spoke to the group. "Remove yourselves from the chamber. When Sanura emerges, she will be our sister or her tongue will be removed so our secrets may never be shared."

CHAPTER 10

Sanura

S anura dug her nails into her palms behind her back, schooling her face into neutrality. *Do not show weakness. Do not show fear*, she chanted in her mind as each coven member dipped their chin and trailed back down the long corridor until only Sanura and Pythia remained.

Pythia held out a hand, beckoning Sanura forward.

She stepped closer, taking comfort in the cool, dead stone under her feet. It steadied her and gave her hope.

"You will face a series of challenges today," Pythia explained. "You must demonstrate your ability with each of the four elements to be accepted into our coven. Do you understand?"

Sanura nodded, shifting from foot to foot.

"A witch is strong, but only one who possesses all four elemental gifts may join our coven. If you lack these skills, there is no shame in turning back now."

Sanura squeezed her fists tighter, relishing the sharp bite of pain as blood welled under her nails. "I understand, Pythia."

"I ask you once more, do you wish to turn back?"

Sanura shook her head even as the contents of her stomach barreled up her throat, threatening to escape.

"Very well." Pythia turned, moving to a stone dais at the center of the room. Lifting one finger, an amber flame flared to life, and she touched it to a bundle of herbs. "Accept the essence of Salvia Divinorum and speak only truth."

Sanura inhaled shallowly, fighting the pull of the smoke growing thick in the chamber. She let the clean air settle in her lungs as she prepared to hold her breath for the next several minutes. She had practiced this many times at home, and though her mother had no explanation for her strange ability, they agreed it would be her best defense for keeping a clear mind.

Pythia's eyes glazed as the drug took hold of her senses. "Now remove all worldly possessions and stand bare before me."

Sanura disrobed, squeezing her fingers tightly to fight the urge to cover herself. In a mind-addled state, nudity should not concern her. She focused on presenting a facade of drugged indifference.

"Very good. First, show me air."

Sanura held her hands out in front of her and blew, pushing all the air from her lungs until the thick fog in the room cleared and the burning pile of herbs was snuffed out.

Pythia's eyes widened as she took in the room, now clear of smoke. "Impressive," she said woozily. She turned, heading back to the pool, and Sanura followed.

"Next, show me your mastery of water."

Sanura leaned forward, touching her finger to the pool's placid surface. Pythia opened her mouth, but Sanura pressed her fingers beneath the water. In the darkness, the ice forming along her fingertips wasn't visible as she pushed chunk after chunk of ice down to the bottom of the pool. As the water rippled, shrinking away from her, she lifted her fingers. Ice exploded from deep below the surface, sending water splashing into the air. It cascaded down around them, and she threw her head back, staring up at the droplets raining down around them.

As she'd hoped, Pythia followed her gaze up to the ceiling as water splashed her cheeks. She glanced at Sanura, grinning, and Sanura's stomach dropped as chunks of ice bobbed along the water's surface.

"What is my next task, Pythia?"

Pythia turned away from the pool, and Sanura's shoulders sagged as she moved to a bare patch of ground. "Earth."

Sanura moved beside her, stretching her fingers wide as she searched below the soil for long dead tree roots and called to them. Brittle cracked wood shot from the ground, racing toward her with such ferocity that she jumped back, narrowly avoiding being impaled by them. In the dark, they could have easily been mistaken for living roots, and a wide grin broke over Pythia's face. She wiped her palms against her pebbled skin and stepped back. Even before Pythia said it, a chill shot down her back. This was the one she feared.

"Fire," Pythia breathed into the room. As if in answer to her summons, crimson flames seemed to stretch toward them from their place along the wall.

Sanura closed her eyes and prayed to whichever God was listening that her plan would work. She blinked her eyes open, glancing left to ensure she'd positioned herself close enough. Then, lifting her hands, palms up, she walked forward. Inhaling sharply, she sucked the air from the room, and the flames rimming them dimmed. Exhaling the oxygen she'd trapped in her lungs in a straight line to her palm, she begged the flames to obey. A red streak shot from the wall into her palm, devouring the only air in the room, and roared to life just above her open hand.

Sanura nearly fainted with relief when fire crackled in her palm for several moments before she expelled the air from her lungs and closed her palms, letting the flames wink out. She squeezed her fingers into fists, hiding the evidence of its burn, and held completely still as she waited for Pythia's next words.

Pythia swayed on her feet, but after a moment, she blinked, her teeth glinting in the low light. She rushed forward, wrapping Sanura in a tight embrace. "Welcome to the coven! Let us choose your new name."

CHAPTER 11

Sanura

Every witch cheered as one as Sanura stumbled out of the dark underground room to find her new coven lounging among angelic statues.

Leontia rushed forward, scrutinizing her. "If you have a tongue, speak your name to your sisters."

"I'm... Persephone."

Everyone cheered once more, calling out her coven name again and again.

"Looks like you do have a bit of magic in those fingers, Cousin," Helena said, bumping her shoulder.

Pythia joined them, and Helena squealed as she pulled both into a close hug. "Let's tell her about Dina first," she said excitedly, tugging Sanura and Pythia to the statue across from the beautiful man. She was tall with elegant features, and something in her nose and chin reminded Sanura of Leontia.

"We're the coven of Dina because the Gavras line descends from her blood."

Pythia rolled her eyes, her vision growing more focused the longer she was above ground.

"We're not all Dina's offspring," she explained. "I'm of Raphael's line and," she pointed to a witch who had introduced herself as Hestia, "she's of Zadkiel's."

"But..." Helena laughed.

"Yeah, okay, but almost everyone else is Dina's."

"What do you mean?" Sanura asked, her forehead wrinkling.

"We're half angels," Helena laughed. "You too. You have all four elemental gifts. Not that you make it obvious."

"I don't understand," Sanura said. "Angels?"

Helena grabbed Sanura's arm, spinning her around in a circle. "We're Nephilim, direct blood relations to the angels. But you can't be a Nephilim even with angel grandparents or great grandparents or, you know, someone in your line unless you can control all four elemental magics." She shrugged as if her words made sense.

"But..." Sanura stumbled back, her head spinning. She'd known she needed to get into this coven, to learn their secrets, to harness the magic and bring it back to her people, but nothing they said made sense. Angels weren't real.

Leontia moved to stand beside them. "Girls. Give us a moment?"

Helena and Pythia exchanged glances before they burst into giggles and darted away.

Leontia rested a hand on Sanura's shoulder and faced her. "I know it's a lot to take in, but I promise you, it's true."

Sanura shook her head. "And only women can be Nephilim?"

Leontia smiled. "No. Lysander and Erasmos are Nephilim, as well. And Aesop. Only Georgios was not born Nephilim. Athena knows why."

Sanura swallowed, gaze trailing to the imposing sculptures lining their path. "How do you know?"

"Come. Walk with me, and I will tell you."

Sanura let Leontia tug her forward as they moved between statues, and she studied them, reveling in the sweet taste on her tongue that always told her when someone spoke true.

"When I was a girl, I knew there was something different about me," Leontia began. "One day, a woman dressed all in white visited me. Her hair held a soft silver sheen, and her iridescent eyes spoke of her immortality. She told me I was her descendant. Offspring of her great, great, great, well, you understand.

"She told me I would be a defender for the people of my city, that I must marry a man of equally pure blood and bring about an age of power for our kind.

"Great evil was coming. A war that would end life as we knew it, and it would be up to my line to ensure Nephilim were strong enough to fight for the humans." She turned, facing Sanura. "Don't you see? Power like yours and mine, it's rare. It inspires hope in the people. We protect them from the evils they cannot see."

Ice slid down Sanura's spine.

Leontia's mouth curved up. "I knew it the moment we met. You feel the darkness, as I do. I hear its call."

Sanura backed up, pulling free from Leontia's grasp.

"It's nothing to fear, child," Leontia continued. "Our gifts tell us of the evil hiding among us so that we may defend against it. You will be of great use to our coven. I think you feel it even more strongly than I do."

Sanura's chest buzzed, heat sliding down her arms to her fingers. She *could* feel it. All around her, death called—screamed for her attention. In her agitated state, she struggled to control it, and small bodies lifted from their dark corners, scurrying toward her. They raced for her, converging at her feet.

Leontia looked down and gasped. "Look how the insects are drawn to you. Just as I was. You are bursting with life, Sanura. Don't fear it. Embrace it."

Sanura stumbled along behind her cousin and aunt, feeling the death around her more keenly than she had in a long time. Leontia was right about one thing: Sanura's power only seemed to grow. Surrounded by these powerful witches—Nephilim—it hummed under her skin. Soon, she would need to release it. If she did not, the dead would find her.

They reached their home as the moon drifted lazily into the sky, and Sanura moved on silent feet to her room. She undid her broach, tugged her simple gold band from thick curls, and slid a light cotton garment over her head.

Lying in bed, she stared at a ceiling of dead bark and clay. She could pull it down on them all, flatten them where they lay, and end every living thing in this house. Some part of her desperately wanted to.

She sat up, tossing back her covers.

Listening for any sounds of life below, she moved to the window and peered at the inky night. Under the cover of darkness, no one would see her. No one would know her secret. She wrapped a shawl loosely around her shoulders, crept down the hall to the stairs, and crossed the courtyard. At the arched entrance, she paused, listening for signs of her uncle. When she heard none, she slipped out into the night.

Letting the pull of death carry her up a steep path beyond their house to a small burial ground at the top of the hill, she exhaled a long sigh. Where death was peaceful, life disrupted the natural order of things, creating chaos as it thrashed across the earth, only finding rest in the end. Solace was what she craved tonight. The tranquility that came with death.

Sliding down beside a large cypress tree, Sanura closed her eyes and let the call of the dead beneath her whisper their desires. They craved an ear to hear their final wish, a hand to hold in their last moment, eyes to set upon them one last time. One by one, she woke them, bringing them forth to grant one last reprieve. Slowly, her heart settled into quiet contentment. Her twisted use of gifts, so unlike the others, had taxed her body and soul. This would put it right.

"Sanura?"

She flew up, wrapping her shawl tightly around herself as she peered into the dark. Stumbling backward, she gasped as glowing blue eyes met hers from the inky darkness.

"Who... Who are you?"

CHAPTER 12

Sanura

Dead branches cracked underfoot as a dark shadow fell over Sanura, and she took another step back. "Don't come near me."

Hands flew out of the shadows placatingly, and Ba'al stepped into the light. "Sanura. It's me."

She sagged against the tree, sighing as she drank him in.

He moved closer, and some invisible force tugged her forward.

She pressed a hand to his broad chest, steadying herself as she looked up at him. Her breath caught. They had spent ten days on a boat together, and yet each time she saw him, it was as if she were laying eyes on him for the first time. How had she ever compared him to the stone sculpture in the temple? He was infinitely more beautiful than the desolate angel with wide wings. He was perfection in human form.

She pressed back, gazing up at him. "How are you here?"

His perfectly carved lips tipped up. "Your magic called me, and I came."

"What?"

He stepped forward, wrapping his large hands around hers. "I've been so worried about you. I wanted to find you, to be sure the witches hadn't harmed you," he whispered. "How are you faring? Are they treating you well?"

Sanura tugged her fingers free from his grasp, stepping back, and his face fell. "I saw you," she said. "I thought I saw you. In the market. But when I searched for you, you were gone. I've searched for you for days. Where have you been?" She blinked. "And what do you mean, my magic called to you?"

Ba'al moved, closing the distance between them. "Sanura, I've been desperate without you. You must know."

Her head swam, his words jumbling together as his nearness set her heart racing, and all her thoughts became lust-filled images of them—tangled in many compromising positions.

"I..."

His mouth crashed against hers, stealing her words, and she melted into him, letting his warm embrace envelop her. His lips parted, and his tongue swept into her mouth.

She panted as a jolt of strange energy raced through her and threw her arms around him.

He groaned, wrapping strong arms around her waist, and lifted her up. They devoured each other, mouths drinking the very air from one another in a dance of give and take as they touched, and something in Sanura's soul welcomed him into her heart.

She sucked his tongue, feeling a strange groove along its center. It wrapped around hers, stroking in a way she never imagined a tongue could, and warmth exploded at her core, licking down her thighs. He tasted like cinnamon and fire and her skin burned everywhere his tongue touched.

The earth rumbled below their feet, and she pulled her mouth from his, leaning back, letting the night breeze cool her cheeks.

Ba'al trailed kisses down her neck and chest, burning a path over flaming skin as he moved down her body. One of his hands slid up her waist, wrapping around her until his fingers found her peaked nipple through fabric and pinched.

Her heart raced as his lips slid her thin nightgown down, and he ran his tongue over her breast, making wet skin pebble before his warm mouth continued south. Terror shot through her when her mind cleared and she suddenly realized where she was—what she was doing.

"Wait." She released him, letting her hands slide down muscled shoulders. "I can't do... this."

Ba'al's grip loosened, and he set her down. The earth settled, some of the angry spirits awoken by her momentary loss of control sliding back into silent stillness as her flaming skin cooled.

"I'm sorry. It's just that we're not..."

Burning ice-blue eyes searched her face, intense desire blazing in them for a moment before the heat banked, and the color returned to that almost human blue they'd always been.

She gasped. "What... What are you?"

"I'm an angel."

CHAPTER 13

Sanura

"I don't think an angel would kiss like that," Sanura said, backing away.

Bright teeth flashed in the dark, and Ba'al stalked closer.

She stumbled over the gnarled roots of the cypress tree behind her, landing hard on the dirt. Where her hands pressed into the ground, dead roots crested the earth, rough bark caressing her palms. She scrambled back, glimpsing a thick fog stretching the confines of Ba'al's skin. His eyes were bright again, glowing in the inky darkness of the night.

"Sanura." Her name was a purr on his lips. "Our fates are bound. You can't escape me. We are inevitable."

"Stop. Ba'al, you're scaring me." She climbed to her feet, wincing as blood welled on her knee, soaking into the fabric of her nightgown. She turned, darting away from him.

In a flash, he was in front of her, and she crashed into his solid chest. Silken fabric bunched under her palms as she balled her fists, prepared to call on the death around her for aid.

"My love, I would never hurt you."

His soothing words calmed her racing heart, quelling some of her terror. Slowly, her gaze lifted, running over his new clothes—made of the finest obsidian silk—to the firm line of his chiseled jaw. She met his unnatural blue eyes, and her breath caught. Fear melted away as the overwhelming desire to lose herself in his teasing kisses swelled inside her. Her stomach flipped, and she fought the urge to climb his tall form and suck that wicked tongue into her mouth again.

His lips split in a wide grin. "Anything you desire, my lady, is yours."

Those words tasted like honey on her tongue as she lifted onto her toes, hands sliding up silken fabric until she curled her fingers in his glossy golden curls, pressing her mouth to his.

A purr rumbled in his chest, his hands finding her waist again, pulling her closer. *You're mine.*

Sanura choked, tearing her mouth from Ba'al's. "What was that?"

"I spoke into your mind."

She released him, meeting his inhuman eyes as she searched them. "Are you truly an angel?"

"I am."

Sanura struggled in his arms, and his grip loosened. She took several steps away, putting distance between them again, and tugged the sleeves of her nightgown, surveying him. For the first time, she saw how much more than a man he was. He'd masked it somehow before—or her gifts were becoming stronger. She couldn't say which had opened her eyes to the truth. Perhaps it was only that she'd learned about angelic beings that day. A thing often became clear only after you knew its secrets.

"The other witches said they had angel blood as well," she began. "Was that the reason you warned me against them? Did you know what they were? You needn't worry. They think I have the same gifts."

Ba'al moved, nearly gliding as he closed the distance between them again. "You're nothing like those witches."

She twisted the end of her sleeve around her arm, tightening it until it was painful, then unwrapping it. "I know. I don't have their abilities."

He hooked a finger under her chin and tipped it up. "Sanura, your gifts are infinitely more impressive than theirs. You command the night and everything that rests among its shadows."

A thrill of nervous energy raced up her spine. No one but her mother and father knew her secret. His words soothed something deep inside her. A long-carried shame for her differences from the rest of the world. It was at once terrifying and freeing to be unburdened by it.

Ba'al wrapped his arms around her again and pulled her against his chest. Unlike before, he didn't kiss her—didn't press his lip to her heated skin and ignite the flames inside her. Instead, he offered comfort, and as he held her, all her fears melted away.

"Why didn't you tell me any of this before?" she whispered.

You weren't ready to hear it.

The words were sweet inside her mind, deeper somehow and more melodic, but they woke a quiet part of her that had lain dormant all her life. An aching longing to be whole in a way she couldn't name. If she'd never met him, she might have never known it was there, but now, it was awake. And Sanura would never be the same.

"I must return. My family—my village—needs me to learn their secrets." They had kissed until Sanura's lips were swollen and the taste of him lingered in her mouth. She pressed her palms against the silken fabric of Ba'al's tunic. It was unlike anything she'd ever seen a man wear. But he wasn't a man.

"They're dangerous, love," he said. "If you remain with them, they will learn of your true gifts." He stroked her cheek, arm tightening around her waist, and she pushed harder against his chest.

"I passed their test." Even as she said the words, thoughts of how close she'd come to failing circled in her mind. Sweat slicked her palms as she wondered how different her life would already be if she had failed. Tongueless and covenless, unable to return home in her shame, she would be like the beggars at the market, cast out and in rags.

Ba'al's soft finger trailed her jawline and ran down her throat, tracing her collarbone until it skimmed the edge of her nightgown.

She shoved him, and this time he released her. "I have to go," she said hurriedly. "They'll notice I'm gone."

Ba'al watched her, saying nothing.

As she stepped back, an ache began in her chest. She took another step and gasped as pain tore through her. It was a knife, spearing her breast and puncturing her heart.

Ba'al moved, wrapping an arm around her, and the ache receded.

She sucked in a breath, inhaling around the ache as it dimmed to a whisper and finally disappeared. "What... was... that?"

"I'm sorry, my love, but we've spent too much time in one another's company. To be parted now is to invite torment," Ba'al explained.

Everywhere he touched her, it cooled her agonized skin, and she leaned into it. "I don't understand."

"We're meant to be together. For eternity. Our fates are one. If you leave me, it will be like this every time."

Sanura grimaced, echoes of the pain from moments before radiating through her. "But I must return to them."

He nodded. "Come, I'll walk you home. The pain will only last until we are too far apart to feel one another."

Sanura wrapped her hands around his and extracted herself from his hold. "It's cruel. Why must we endure it?" The moment she'd pried his fingers free, she felt his absence. Her body craved him—her chest spasming in some silent plea to remain in his arms.

"It's a long story, one we don't have time for this night," he said. "For now, I'll say this: It was a punishment meted out by my father for the actions of my sibling. One we all must bear."

"Your father?"

Ba'al turned to face her, leaning down to cup her cheeks and planting a kiss on her forehead. "I will tell you more when next we meet. The sun will rise soon."

She nodded, glancing past him to the sliver of red rimming the distant horizon. "Stay here," she said. "I'll go. If this pain lessens with distance, I'll need to recover before I make it through the courtyard. Please, Ba'al, go the other way."

His eyes searched hers, sky blue in the rapidly lightening morning, and he nodded. "Meet me tonight?"

Her brows dipped. "I'll be up all day. I need sleep."

He frowned but nodded again. "Tomorrow then. Now go. Hurry."

She turned, staggering away from him as pain sliced through her, and she doubled over, retching beside the road. Righting herself, she took one unsteady step after another, and finally, as he'd promised, when she reached the bottom of the hill, the pain leached from her body until it was only a memory.

CHAPTER 14

Sanura

S anura reached the courtyard of the Gavras home just as golden pre-dawn light spilled across the doorframe. She slipped inside and wrapped her shawl tightly around her shoulders. Creeping past the kitchen, she heard the house staff already awake and preparing for their day. She stopped outside the door, peeking in, and rushed by when she was sure no one was turned in her direction. She did the same as she passed several more doors on the first floor, setting a hand on the smooth wooden railing and stepping up.

"What do you think you're doing?"

Sanura spun around, heart in her throat, and stared up at bleary red eyes pinning her in place.

"Uncle." She swallowed, backing up the first step as he marched over dirt, stopping inches from her.

His sour breath burned her nostrils, and he tilted forward, pressing his massive girth into her chest. "Where have you been? Out with a man? Not so different from your whore of a mother, are you?"

She leaned backward, the hard edge of the stairs against her back.

He pressed closer, his weight pushing her harder into the sharp-edged wood. "You smell like you've been tumbling in the hay." He raised a hand overhead. "I'll teach you the lesson my father never taught your mother." His hand swung, flying so fast she wasn't prepared for it; stars exploded across her vision when it crashed into her cheek. Something cracked on the wood beside her, but her mind was having trouble making sense of it.

Throbbing started in her ear, and she only had time to open her eyes before another wave barreled into her. Dimly, she was aware of the weight atop her as she slid down the stairs to the ground and pain exploded through the other side of her face. Someone far away was screaming, but the shrill sound and her agony faded, replaced by darkness and calm. The world was black.

Her last thought before consciousness left her was of the cool, skeletal fingers wrapping around hers.

Sanura cracked one eye as light filtered through her lashes and came into focus in shades of red. A blurry shape moved, and her body dipped with the ground beneath her as warmth radiated at her side.

"Where am..." she whispered through cracked lips.

"Shhh. Don't speak, Sanura."

Cool dampness settled on her forehead, and she winced at the pain radiating from her skull.

"Water?" The blurry object solidified into the shape of her cousin as she reached past her and brought a cup to her mouth.

Sanura sighed as the cool liquid touched her lips, wetting her sticky tongue and washing away a lingering metallic taste.

Helena set the cup on a low table beside them and slowly, the room came into focus. She was in her cousin's bed in the Gavras home.

Sanura struggled to sit up, but Helena laid a gentle hand on her shoulder and pressed her down. "Mother wanted to wait till you were awake to heal you, but don't move too much, okay?"

Sanura blinked back burning tears that threatened to cloud her vision again. That night was a dark, shadowed memory, but one thing was burned into her thoughts—etched into her soul. Tears were quickly replaced by rage as Antyamos's meaty palm connecting with her cheek flashed in her mind. He hit her. Not once. Not twice. He hadn't even stopped when her head cracked against the sharp edge of the stairs. She counted four strikes before her thoughts had become too muddled to separate new aches from old ones.

She lifted trembling fingers to her ear and bit down hard on her lip when a stinging pain nearly turned her stomach. Her fingers came away wet, and she held them in front of her face.

"I'll get Mother. Don't try to move." Helena stood, darting from the room.

Sanura said nothing, twisting her fingers as she stared in morbid fascination at the dark, congealed globs of blood stuck to her fingertips. He had done this. He had made her bleed.

Leontia came in quietly, her presence barely disturbing the air. She sat beside Sanura and leaned close. "My sweet child, how are you faring?"

A rumbling fury burbled up Sanura's chest. Cold rage simmered in her veins, begging for freedom, begging to be released upon their entire family. She balled her hands into fists, the clumpy wetness of her blood squishing against her palms.

"How am I faring?" she seethed, biting out each word. She slid her elbows under her, lifting to meet the matron's gaze—locking the pain pounding in her skull behind a wall. Her eyes narrowed. "How would you feel after a man who was charged with your care beat you until you were unconscious?" Her arms trembled under her weight, but she pushed onto her palms, sitting up even as the room spun.

Leontia's eyes widened, and she leaned back. All her confident grace fled her as the scent of fear doused the room.

It quelled the ice creeping up Sanura's veins, and she collapsed onto the bed, crying out as mind-numbing pain radiated from the side of her head.

The matron shuddered but masked it quickly, cupping her palms and bringing them forward. Sanura shrank back, but Leontia brought her cupped hands over her ear. A soft light burst from her palms, warmth soaking into her skin. It burned and seared the tender flesh along her earlobe, but in moments, tension bled from her as the pain receded and her thoughts cleared.

Leontia's palms fell away, and chill air bit into the still-aching wound. "This will take more than one session, I'm afraid," she said. "It was more severe than I knew. With head injuries, it's best to wait until the patient can tell me where it hurts most."

That admission dulled some of the rage Sanura felt for the woman. She wondered how many times the matron had to heal these types of wounds on her own children.

Leontia's gaze dropped, and she stood.

Sanura's hand shot out, wrapping around her wrist. "I'm sorry. You're not to blame for his actions."

The matron's eyes blurred, and she nodded once, looking away. "I'll be back to check on you soon. Helena will bring food." Silently, she moved out of the room.

Sanura watched her go, emotions warring with one another. When the matron was gone and she was alone, the bitter hatred lingering on her tongue dissolved, and silent tears streaked down her cheeks.

CHAPTER 15

Sanura

Helena slid into the bed beside Sanura, careful not to touch her. Sanura kept her eyes closed, her breathing steady.

Helena had been in and out of the room more than a dozen times that day, and her insufferable doting had worsened each time. On her fifth visit, Sanura had been dozing when Helena rushed in and crashed to a stop. The sound had woken her, but she knew then that her cousin would only grant her a respite when she slept, so she faked it for the rest of the afternoon and into the evening.

Leontia brought her dinner and sat silently, lifting a spoon to her lips until the simple broth the kitchen had prepared especially for her was gone. Then she'd cupped her palms over Sanura's injury again, and the warmth of her healing magic further stitched her wound together. When she finished, Leontia left, saying nothing, and Sanura closed her eyes once more.

Now, in the silent stillness of the night, only Helena, tossing and turning beside her, disturbed her peace.

"Aniel," Helena mumbled.

Sanura turned, but Helena's flaxen lids were glued against her cheeks. She rolled to her side, away from her cousin, sliding an arm under her head, and closed her eyes again. Blinding light seared the backs of her eyelids, an intense glow engulfing the room before it dimmed suddenly. The shape of a man—not a man, a creature—with enormous white wings appeared in Helena's room.

Behind her, Helena tumbled out of bed and raced to him, throwing herself into his arms. "Aniel. I'm so glad you came." Her gaze darted to Sanura. "But it's not the best time to visit. My cousin is sleeping with me for a little while."

His melodic chuckle was intoxicating as it drifted through the room on a phantom breeze. "Your cousin is awake, my dove."

Sanura started, eyes flying wide, and Helena pulled free from the creature's arms and dropped to her knees beside Sanura on the floor.

"Please, Cousin, you mustn't say anything," she pleaded. "Father would kill me."

Sanura's gaze darted to the snowy wings behind Helena's creature, dazzling even in the darkness, and back to her cousin. "I will not share your secrets."

Helena grabbed her hands, squeezing. "Thank you. I owe you."

Sanura's heart twisted, understanding somewhat better why her cousin had been so fearful before. She'd known her uncle was abrasive, but she hadn't understood the depth of his ruthlessness until today. "You owe me nothing." She offered Helena a tentative smile.

Helena climbed to her feet and turned back to her lover. He wrapped his arms around her, beaming at Sanura, and scooped Helena up. He turned, stepping through the window, and his wings spread wide as they dipped before lifting into the sky.

Sanura slid out of bed, moving on unsteady legs to the window. A dull ache throbbed in her temple, but she felt remarkably better than before Leontia's second healing. She searched the sky for any sign of the pair, but murky grey clouds obscured her view, and moonless as it was, she saw nothing.

Sanura woke to the soft snores of her cousin beside her and morning light streaming across her face. Stretching her arms overhead, she winced at the bruising on her back she hadn't noticed when her head injury had overwhelmed her senses. She sat up gingerly, bare feet touching cool, dead wood. It sent energy through her, lending her strength, and she moved toward the door.

"Sanura."

She turned, facing her cousin.

"I'm sorry about Father," Helena said. "Next time you want to sneak out, let me know. I'll show you how to come in through the window."

Sanura searched her cousin's sleep-rumpled form, wondering how many times Leontia had healed her injuries until none remained but those she carried on her soul. "I won't sneak out again."

Helena rubbed her eyes and opened her mouth to say more, but Sanura turned and left before she could.

In her room, Sanura dressed quickly, stuffing only what she brought with her into her bag and tugging her worn, threadbare shawl over her crimson curls. Reaching under the bed, she pulled out the small hand mirror she'd brought to ward the room of evil and slid it in among her clothes.

"He won't touch you again."

Sanura spun, heart leaping into her throat, and met Leontia's hazel-eyed gaze. She clutched her bag to her chest. "I know," Sanura said. "Because I won't let him."

Leontia stepped into the room, nodding. "Neither will I."

Sanura swallowed, her fingers tightening around her bag. She tracked the matron's slow movement, shoulders tensing.

She stopped in front of Sanura. "You came to learn about your magic. If you leave now, you'll be walking away from your only opportunity to gain that knowledge from us. There aren't many Nephilim."

Sanura's shoulders loosened, eyes darting to the door.

Leontia held her arm up, revealing a thin white line running the length of her forearm.

Sanura's gaze snagged on its uneven edges before darting back to Leontia's face.

"I underestimated him once. I could have left, gone back to my parents, and accepted defeat. But that day, I decided no man would choose my fate." Her hazel eyes searched Sanura's golden ones.

FATED

"Do you want to give a man that kind of power over yours?"

CHAPTER 16

Sanura

S anura swallowed. Her gaze darted back to Leontia's scar. Some of the ice that had crept up her veins before resurfaced, coating the tips of her fingers. She realized then she wasn't angry with Leontia for not protecting her. She was angry with Leontia for allowing the man to live.

"We could kill him." The words had slipped off her tongue, and she couldn't take them back. Sanura backed up, chest pounding. Leontia had scolded her son for merely *speaking* against his father. What would she do to the girl who threatened his life?

Leontia's eyes narrowed a fraction before her lips stretched into a wide grin, and she laughed.

Some of the tension in Sanura's posture relaxed, and she let slip a tentative smile.

Leontia closed the distance between them and held up her hands. "May I?"

Sanura flinched.

Leontia kept her hands outstretched, waiting for permission.

Sanura nodded, arms falling to her sides. Light glowed under the matron's cupped palms. Sanura leaned into her touch, sighing as healing magic revived dead skin and stitched itself together.

"Are you injured anywhere else?"

Sanura twisted around. "My lower back."

Leontia undid her ties, letting her tunic part to expose her back, and inhaled sharply. "Go lay down, child. I'll heal this as well."

Sanura obeyed, dropping her bag beside the bed.

"You may have trouble controlling your magic for a time," Leontia explained. "Head injuries this severe can affect your gifts. I've healed the superficial damage, but there's more below the surface. I can feel it."

Sanura cast a sideways glance at the matron. "Will that affect my place in the coven?"

Leontia's warm fingers traced a line down Sanura's back, making her shudder. "No, child. I will tell our sisters that you fell. They will understand."

The words soured something in Sanura's stomach. The implication was clear. These women were used to injuries among their kind, and they, too, would turn a blind eye to it. Icy anger slid down her spine again, chasing away Leontia's healing touch.

Sanura slipped into her seat beside Helena at the breakfast table and lifted her cup to her lips with trembling fingers. Silent terror coated the room; Sanura knew it was hers. Leontia had assured her Antyamos had not come home since the incident, choosing to stay at the Acropolis. But every step down the stairs—no longer painted with her blood—sent her heartbeat into a frenzy, and now her eyes kept darting to the door.

Sweat beaded her brow, and Helena tossed a sympathetic glance her way every time another member of the house staff entered to set something out on the table.

She nearly sprung from her seat when heavy footfall sounded in the courtyard and a long shadow stretched into the room.

When Lysander stepped through the doorway, she heaved a sigh of relief. Even Leontia stared at her. Lysander's gaze met hers, and a heat that matched Sanura's icy fury blazed in his eyes. He crossed the room, breaking tradition, and sat beside her.

"How are you?" he asked. "Are you feeling better?" He slid a hand across the table, but she flinched back. His look was filled with so much sorrow and regret that she almost felt sorry for *him*.

Shame bubbled up inside her. She had hoped the others didn't know what happened to her. Had hoped they thought she'd taken ill or some other mysterious thing. She saw now how futile that hope had been.

"I'm so sorry, Sanura. He'll never lay a hand on you again. I promise."

She dropped her gaze, unable to meet his eyes, and swallowed the humiliation rising higher in her chest. *It wasn't my fault*, she reminded herself, but in the harsh light of day, with all the pitying looks thrown her way, she thought she would be sick.

Lysander stretched his hand out again, and she shot up from her seat, backing up. "Excuse me, Matron. I'm not feeling quite myself this morning. I wish to be excused."

"Of course, Sanura," Leontia replied. "I will have Agetha bring something to your room."

Sanura nodded, fighting the tears threatening to give away her weakness, and dashed from the room, swiping her cheeks as she reached the courtyard.

"Sanura. Wait." Lysander called after her.

Leontia's low voice carried into the courtyard, but she couldn't make out the words. Lysander didn't follow.

She threw open the door to her room, closed it behind her, and slid to the floor, wrapping her arms around her knees as she let the tears fall.

When the sobs quieted, she rubbed her cheeks and climbed to her feet. A knock came at the door, and Sanura's heart leaped into her throat. "Yes?"

"I have breakfast, my lady."

She opened the door and took the tray from a woman she assumed must be Agetha.

"Thank you."

Agetha nodded and backed up, moving briskly back down the hall.

Sanura closed the door and brought the tray to her bed, setting it down just as another knock sounded. "Come in."

She looked up to find Leontia pressing the door wide. "We have a meeting with the coven today. Are you up for it?"

Sanura swallowed a bite of bread and flattened her palm against her soft blanket. If she planned to stay, this was why she was here. She couldn't hide from the world and their consoling looks. She would have to hold her head high and show them she wouldn't be cowed by violence. Nodding, she tore another piece of bread from the loaf, biting into it.

Leontia gave her an assessing look. "Lysander was the one who pulled him off you. I would not have told him."

Sanura choked, looking up.

"I know the rage that burns within a woman when a man lays his hands on her. I know the outlet she seeks. I only wish to impart that I'm not your enemy. Direct your rage to the person who deserves it. And Sanura," she tilted her chin, meeting Sanura's eyes. "We look out for one another in this family."

CHAPTER 17

Sanrua

Sanura ran a clammy palm down silken emerald fabric as she raced after Helena and Leontia.

"Remember to call me Aphrodite and Mother Dianna. We don't use real names here," Helena called over her shoulder.

Sanura stumbled over a rock and crashed to her knees. A hand slid under her elbow, lifting her. She looked up, meeting bright sapphire eyes, and gasped. She peered into the distance, seeing Helena's golden curls bounce as she raced through the pillars several feet ahead.

"Where have you been?" Ba'al hissed. His tone held a bite to it, and Sanura's hackles rose.

"I was dealing with a family matter," she bit back.

"I waited in the cemetery for three nights and went to the market looking for you." He searched her face, golden brows dipping low as he gripped her jaw, twisting her head to the side. "Who did that to you?"

The icy menace in his tone sent a chill down her spine, and she tore her chin from his grasp. "I fell."

She wasn't sure why she'd lied to him, but the energy rolling off Ba'al was equally thrilling and terrifying, and she half expected him to burst into flames and consume her in his rage.

"Don't lie to me," he seethed. "Name the offender, and his life shall be mine."

Sanura met his cold stare with a glacial one of her own. "If anyone is owed revenge, it's me."

"Who was it?"

Antyamos flashed in her mind, and a wicked smile crept over Ba'al's face.

"He draws his last breath tonight."

Another jolt of frost shot down her spine at the absolute promise in his words. They were honey on her tongue, and she knew he spoke the truth.

"Sanura?"

Sanura glanced in the direction of her cousin's voice.

Warmth evaporated at her side, and when she turned back, Ba'al was gone; it was as if he were made of smoke. Angel, she reminded herself.

Helena appeared ahead, and her cousin's creature with broad, snowy wings flashed in her mind. Somehow, she expected an angel to look more like that.

Helena reached her side and looped her arm through Sanura's. "Cousin, what happened to you? You look as though you've seen a devil." She laughed, tugging Sanura up the stairs leading to the hall of angelic sculptures.

Sanura darted a glance over her shoulder to the darkened corners lining their walk, feeling eyes on her, but saw no one.

At the end of the long corridor, Leontia pressed stones in the same pattern as before. A hole opened in the floor as stairs stretched into the earth. They descended silently, their path lit by pink flame, a nervous thrill racing through Sanura as they reached the bottom.

"It's a crescent moon on the equinox—a very auspicious time," Helena whispered. "Our Pythia will share a vision with us tonight."

In the middle of the room, her new sisters sat in a perfect circle, and at its center, Pythia writhed and moaned, dancing to a silent tune. Sage and another herb Sanura couldn't place burned on the dais. The room was thick with oppressive smoke. Sanura breathed shallowly, fighting its effects.

Helena and Leontia found their places in the circle, and she slid down beside them. They swayed, humming softly. All around her, magic hung heavy in the air. Each communed with their elemental gifts, channeling them through their body and sending them into the circle.

Pythia accepted their offerings, absorbing them. Her movements, graceful and erotic, transfixed Sanura. Something stirred low in her belly, a heady, sensual feeling, compelling her to sway with them. Her skin warmed, begging to be freed of her oppressive clothing, and she lifted a hand, trailing it over emerald fabric, up her peaked nipples to her collarbone, and slid the fabric down overheated flesh.

"Get your mental shield up, Cousin," Helena whispered sharply, jarring Sanura back to her senses.

She tugged her clothes over her shoulder and exhaled, expelling the noxious fumes from her lungs. Blinking several times, she glanced around the circle, noticing now that most of the witches used some form of magic to keep the poisoned fumes at bay.

Only their Pythia, writhing at its center, gave into the drug, letting it funnel through her. Most of the others had shimmering air shiels around them, but without the traditional gift of air magic to aid her, Sanura could only hold her breath and hope the herbs would burn out soon. Pythia stopped swaying, eyes rolling back in her head. She sank to her knees, a tremor rocking her body, and her head fell forward, obscuring her face.

Sanura slid her gaze around the room. Every witch's focus was locked on their Pythia.

For a long moment, there was nothing but silence and the crackle of burning herbs. Then, Pythia lifted her head.

"Darkness comes," she said. "Darkness and decimation. It coats the Earth in icy fire. A tempest of rage." Her body convulsed, and she slumped forward once more.

Sanura shot a nervous glance around the room, but the others remained transfixed.

Pythia looked up again, eyes rolled back so only the whites were exposed. "Theirs is a love that will devour the world. Fear it, for it will be our end." She collapsed to the ground, and the fire encircling the room winked out.

CHAPTER 18

Sanura

When Pythia rose from her stupor, the wall sconce blazed to life, chased by a stream of fire, bathing the room in a soft yellow glow. The herbs were gone from the dais, and several witches worked quickly to clear the lingering fog.

Pythia shakily accepted her sisters' hands as they led her to the bath. She slid into the water with a sigh. The others disrobed and joined her. Sanura slid slick palms over her shoulders, letting her tunic fall to the floor, and climbed in. This time, no one danced or touched one another. No one hummed that siren's tune, and she settled against the cool stone wall, observing them in the dimly lit space.

Helena sloshed through the water, sitting beside her. "What did you think?"

Pythia joined them. "It was a lot for your first time, wasn't it? It's okay. You can say so. We only commune with our angelic line twice a year. It can be overwhelming."

"You spoke with Dina?" Sanura whispered.

"I wouldn't call it speaking *with* her," Pythia said. "I opened myself to receive her message, and she spoke through me."

Sanura's brows furrowed. "How do you know it was Dina?"

"We have devoted ourselves to Dina. She is the only angel who's ever spoken to us."

"How do you know?" Sanura's gaze darted between Helena and Pythia.

They exchanged a look, and Helena said, "That's how it works, Persephone. Our coven was built in honor of Dina, and she guides us."

Sanura gave them both another skeptical look, but Pythia's brows were inching down her forehead, and Sanura sensed their hostility building. She reminded herself she didn't need to believe them, only to learn from them, and nodded slowly.

"I see."

The look on Helena's face told her they hadn't bought her acceptance, but they let it drop. Helena turned to Pythia and said, "What do you think it means? It was so foreboding. But a love that will devour the world... How romantic."

"I know," Pythia gushed. "I mean, could there be a better way to go, Aphrodite?"

"Nope."

The pair giggled, and Sanura fought hard to rein in her disbelief. Was this truly what she was risking her life for? Girls swooning over love matches? No one's love could be that powerful. Even as she thought it, though, Ba'al's lips brushing hers came to her mind, and the ache of his absence pulsed in her chest. A memory of the agony that tore through her when she left him that night in the cemetery danced through her mind. Why hadn't she felt that same pain outside the temple? Had it all been some fever dream? Had she imagined kissing him beneath the moon and stars, wishing she could have done so much more?

"Who do you think it could be about?" Helena asked, cutting into her thoughts.

Sanura blinked, reminding herself she was supposed to be fitting in, learning their secrets. "I'm sorry, what?"

"The lovers. Who do you think they are?" Pythia asked in exasperation.

"I've only just arrived here. I don't know many people."

"It could be you and your mystery man, Aphrodite." Pythia gave Helena a shove, and Helena's grin faltered as her gaze darted across the pool to Leontia. "Pythia. Stop."

Pythia's smile fell a fraction before she turned her attention to Sanura. "What about you, Persephone? Is your Hades coming to set the world ablaze for you?"

Sanura twisted her hands together under the water. Should she tell them about her angel? Would they believe her? She darted a look at Helena as the image of the creature who had appeared in her room flashed through her mind again. Helena's lover wasn't golden-haired or classically handsome like Ba'al, but his silvery wings were on the scale of the sculptures they'd passed on their way down.

Helena's eyes widened as she seemed to register Sanura's train of thought, and she shook her head, eyes pleading.

Sanura opened her mouth.

"Actually, my brother has all but staked his claim on Persephone," she cut in. "Ly—"

"We don't use real names here," Helena spoke loudly, shooting her a murderous glare.

Pythia glanced between them and burst out laughing. "Well, whoever this Lye is, I wonder if his love is enough to devour the world."

Sanura bit her lip, remembering Lysander's hand sliding toward hers at the breakfast table that morning. She needed to find him, to apologize for her actions. He had saved her from his father, and Dionysus only knew what punishment he'd suffered for that. He hadn't deserved her coldness.

Sanura's heart thrummed in her chest as they crested the hill and the Gavras home came into view. She wiped her clammy palms on her tunic, taking another step and exhaling slowly.

Lysander appeared in the arched door frame of their courtyard, and her breathing slowed. His lips split into a wide grin; knowing he'd already forgiven her, Sanura's spirits lifted instantly.

Leontia and Helena slipped by him, Leontia lingering to give him an unreadable look. Lysander ignored it, sweeping past her to meet Sanura on the stone path.

"How was it? How was your meeting with Helena's friends?" He waggled his eyebrows, and her remaining trepidation leeched away. His smile was infectious, and she found herself grinning with him.

"It was strange."

"I've always wondered what the women there do."

She opened her mouth. Closed it.

He nodded. "I know. Coven secrets."

"Your mother told me you're like us," Sanura said. "Do you not have a coven of your own?"

He laughed, closing the distance between them and holding out a hand.

She looked down—her heart launching into her throat— and back up, eyes wild with panic.

He dropped his hand, but his smile never faltered. "Walk with me?" Lysander moved away from the house, and she expelled a relieved sigh. Somehow, he had known she wasn't ready to be trapped under that roof just yet.

They strolled in silence, a calm settling over her. There was no heat or friction between them the way there was with Ba'al—being with Lysander was easy.

He stopped, and she halted beside him. They'd reached the hill's summit. Sanura's breath caught as she took in the city stretched out below. Twinkling lights shone across a great expanse in a near reflection of the night sky.

"It's wondrous."

She glanced back, meeting Lysander's gaze, already on her.

"It's nothing compared with you."

Heat burned in her cheeks, and she silently thanked Nyx for the cover of night concealing her embarrassment.

Lysander moved closer, and she froze in place. He lifted a hand, tangling his fingers in her curls. "Sanura."

She tracked his movement, hardly breathing as he let her curl drop and hooked a finger under her chin, tipping it up.

"You must know how I feel about you." Her gaze met his. "Your beauty ensnared me the moment I laid eyes on you. I think. I think..."

"Lysander." She stepped back—out of his reach. "I know what you did for me. I'm grateful."

His brows furrowed. "But."

"But we hardly know each other."

His gaze softened. "I'm not asking you to be my wife today.

She choked on a laugh. "Did you have another day in mind?"

His face turned serious again. "I did."

She swallowed, eyes dropping to his finely made sandals.

"I only mean... I would be honored if you would consider me."

His feet shuffled on stone, and her lips quirked at his boyish agitation. She looked up, meeting his gaze once more. "I will give your question serious consideration."

The corners of his lips lifted, and Sanura's stomach twisted into knots. He was so kind and thoughtful. He would make some woman a wonderful husband one day. But though she hadn't said it, Sanura feared her heart was already spoken for.

CHAPTER 19

Sanura

Sanura slid under her blanket, feeling lighter than she had in days. Although she would have to let Lysander down soon, tonight, she basked in the comforting warmth of his heartfelt declaration. In her village, men found her odd, dangerous, distasteful. Lysander made her feel none of those things. His was an uncomplicated devotion, lacking prejudice or intolerance, and the kindness he'd shown her since arriving settled over her like a warm caress.

She closed her eyes, sighing.

A tug at her chest woke her. She blinked, searching the room's dark corners for the presence she felt but couldn't see. It crawled over her skin like death always did, but this was something different. "Show yourself."

Red gleaming eyes blinked in the darkness as a shape solidified.

"Who are you?" Sanura asked. "What do you mean by calling on me when I have not summoned you?"

The creature bowed low, showing her the deference all dead things did. "I bring a message." The words slithered between his reptilian lips.

"From whom?" She sat up, narrowing her eyes at him.

"My king."

She squinted, trying to make out the being who had disturbed her. "Come closer. Let me see you."

He moved into the moonlight, and it pierced his insubstantial form, refracting off curved horns and penetrating his middle.

"Who do you claim is your king, and what business does he have with me?"

The creature's horns scraped her floor in another bow. "My king hasss many namesss, but you know him as Ba'al."

Sanura's heart thumped in her chest. Her angel commanded the dead? What could it mean?

"My king bade me bring you glad newsss. He ssslew your enemy thisss night. He alssso bade me ssshare a token of hisss affection."

Something solid thwacked against the floor.

Sanura stared down at the stump of a bloody, meaty hand. Gasping, she leaped from her bed and crouched to examine the palm that had once struck her face hard enough to make her bleed. She nudged it with her toe. It rolled, thick, congealing blood trailing after it. The shadowy creature who had dropped it disappeared, leaving her alone with her gift.

Shuffling outside her room had her looking up, and she grabbed the hand, stuffing it under her bed as her door creaked open and Helena poked her head in.

"Are you okay? I thought I heard... a man." She glanced around the room, then back to Sanura standing beside the bed. "What's that?" She stepped in, closing the distance between them.

Sanura clasped her hands over a dark stain on her nightgown. "What's what?"

Helena pinched the collar of Sanura's nightgown, running it between her fingers. "Is that... blood?" She lifted it, sniffing.

Sanura's heart crashed into an erratic beat in her chest. "It's mine. From when I was injured."

Helena blanched. "I'm so sorry. I only came because I wanted to be sure father hadn't..." the words died on her lips.

Sanura said nothing, eyes going wide as she spied the trail of blood running across her floor and under her bed.

"We all feel awful about what happened," Helena said, drawing her attention back to her. "I want you to know we won't ever let it happen again."

Sanura nodded, a knot of tension forming in her stomach. She needed a cloth and water, but she'd have to get those things without anyone seeing her. Leaving her room at night also meant risking running into... She crossed that thought out, refusing to believe he was truly dead by Ba'al's hand until she had more than his gift to prove it.

Her cousin searched her face. "I wasn't as kind as I should have been when you arrived. I want us to be close. To be sisters."

Sanura nodded again, groaning internally at Helena's persistence. "I want that, too."

Helena beamed at her. "Good. If you want, you can sleep with me."

"No," Sanura said quickly, and Helena's brows dipped. "I sleep better alone." It was a lie, but she would have said anything to chase her cousin from her room. She yawned loudly. "I'm actually quite tired. Could we continue this conversation tomorrow?"

Helena nodded. "Yes. Of course. Get some sleep. I'll see you in the morning." She gave Sanura another once over before turning to leave.

Sanura let out a heavy sigh and crossed the room, leaning against the door to listen for Helena's light footfall as she retreated down the hall. She waited several more moments before cracking it open.

A loud bang downstairs sent her heart into her throat, and she slammed her door closed.

"Mother! Mother, wake up!" Lysander's voice called from the bottom of the stairs. "It's Father. He's dead! Cut down in the street!"

Sanura's heart pounded so hard she thought it might burst from her chest. No time. There was no time to hide the evidence. She stripped her nightgown off and dragged it over the floor, wiping away all traces of her gift. Reaching under the bed, she found the cold, stiff fingers of Antyamos Gavras and pulled them out, wrapping the hand tightly in the fabric of her nightgown and wiping the puddle gathered under her bed. She balled the fabric up and stuffed it at the bottom of her chest, covering it with a deep burgundy blanket.

Her fingers grazed soft cotton, and she tugged out a robe Helena had let her borrow that she'd never returned. She wrapped it around herself, sliding the soft fabric over her shoulder as the door crashed open and Lysander stood in the doorframe. His gaze traveled the length of her, going slowly over her curves, and when his eyes met hers, they blazed with a heat she felt all the way to her core.

She swallowed.

He stepped into the room.

"Lysander?" Leontia's questioning tone cut through the dense haze of lust permeating every surface and doused it in cold water. "What has happened to your father?"

His gaze left hers reluctantly, and he turned to face his mother. "He was found on the street. Stripped of his clothes, then skinned and dragged until he was nearly unrecognizable."

The callous, unfeeling way he delivered the information left Sanura with no doubt he did not mourn the death of his father.

A hand flew to Leontia's mouth.

"They only knew him by his ring."

CHAPTER 20

Sanura

Something cold settled in Sanura's belly. He had done it. For her. Her brutal, avenging angel had found the man who made her bleed and repaid him tenfold. A chilling feeling slithered through her, and she knew what it was. Satisfaction. He'd deserved every moment of whatever torture he had endured; she was only angry she hadn't been the one to deliver it.

Her chest spasmed, a call to her very soul. Her angel was begging her to join him. She looked up, meeting Leontia's gaze. Somehow, Leontia had felt it too.

"I must go," Sanura said.

Leontia dipped her chin.

Lysander glanced between them. "Go where? Sanura, he's dead. You're free of him. We all are."

She rushed past, ignoring him.

"Sanura. Wait."

"Let her go, son." Leontia's words chased her down the hall, the stairs, and through the courtyard. She breached the archway and raced over dirt and stone until she reached the cemetery, stopping beside the old cypress tree and searching the darkness.

An invisible pull in her chest tugged her forward, and she moved again, crashing into the solid form of her angel, staring up at bright blue eyes frozen with desire. "You killed him."

"Yes."

"For me."

"Yes."

Her heart raced, and she raised onto her toes, slinging her arms around his neck. Her mouth found his as he wrapped his arms around her waist and lifted her.

Ba'al hugged her to him, meeting her fervor with the same intensity. They were tongues and teeth and desire, and in that moment, she understood how two people's passion could devour the world.

When he released her, her palms slid down his broad chest until they reached the sharp indentation of his hips, her fingers tracing their grooves south, stopping on the outline of his arousal. It stretched toward her, growing as she ran a soft finger over the fabric separating her from his manhood.

His mouth found hers again, and his long fingers slid up her back, into her hair, and coiled in it. He tugged. Icy desire surged through her as her head tilted backward, exposing her throat.

His lips left hers, trailing kisses down her skin until he reached her breastbone, and his tongue slipped out, splitting in that strange way it had before and licking down her chest.

Sanura's fingers traced the outline of his length, and she cupped her hands over its head. She gasped as the thin fabric separating them dissolved into nothing, slick wetness coating her palm.

"Tell me you're mine," he breathed. His tongue slid farther south, his nose nudging the fabric of her robe aside, exposing her breast to the chill night air.

A breathy moan escaped her as his tongue glided over her nipple, and he bit down gently.

"Tell me you belong to me, Sanura."

Her fingers wrapped around him and stroked.

His lips closed over her sensitive bud, and he sucked, gently at first, then harder. His hand tightened into a fist in her hair, pulling sharply.

She matched his intensity, sliding her hand up and down the length of him until he groaned against her wet nipple.

Ba'al released her hair, his hands tracing a path southward, light touch skimming over thin fabric and cupping her butt in his palms. He lifted her, showing surprising strength as he slid her body down his now bare chest. As her robe fell apart, her legs spread too, and the wetness pooling between her thighs traced a line down his abdomen.

She wrapped her legs around his waist.

Their eyes met, and his—frozen chips of icy desire—searched her face, the desperate longing in his expression mirroring her own sharp need.

She nodded, and it was all the confirmation he needed.

His lips crashed against hers, his grip tightening as he brought her body down, the hard length of him sliding inside her.

Sanura cried out as burning pain tore through her, and she dug her nails into his shoulders, finding purchase as he lifted her and brought her down again. The friction of her sensitive skin rubbing along his smooth abdomen, coupled with his sex filling her so completely, was intoxicating and new.

"You're mine," he groaned, sliding her up and down his body.

Her nails pierced his flesh, warm blood sliding down her fingers as a pleasure she'd never known exploded inside her.

"Tell me." He moved her faster, and the intense feeling built again, clouding her thoughts. "Say it," he growled.

"I'm yours, Ba'al. I'm yours!" She screamed the words as her body convulsed, and Ba'al's teeth sank into her shoulder as she cried out again.

Sanura closed her eyes, reveling in all the new sensations, a dizzying mix of pleasure and pain that threatened to send her over the edge before she'd recovered. When Ba'al's forked tongue ran over the cut in her shoulder and the skin knitted itself together, something in her chest purred.

Ba'al lifted her, and her thighs—slick with wetness—were cold in the absence of him. He set her down on her bare feet and laid out a robe he'd seemingly conjured from thin air.

"Sit with me a while, my love."

Sanura sank to her knees on soft fabric.

He settled himself beside her and lifted her fingers, still coated in his blood. She sucked in a sharp breath as he brought them to her lips, painting them in his blood.

"Your blood is gold?"

"Like your eyes."

She licked her lip, tasting that same cinnamon and fire she had every time they kissed. "What does it mean?"

"That we are meant for one another."

The words held a slight slur and reminded her of his creature's visit only an hour ago. "You are the King of the Dead?"

Ba'al searched her face, sapphire eyes glowing brightly in the pitch night. "Would you fear me if I said yes?"

Sanura let out a soft chuckle. "I would be forced to name myself a pretender for judging you. You've seen my command of them." She cocked an eyebrow, gaze traveling over his shadowy robes. "Yet they have never mentioned you."

Ba'al beckoned her closer, and she leaned against his arm, breath catching as a rush of warmth surged in her chest.

"Your dead and mine are not the same, my love, but you are no less a queen than I am a king."

His words were like honey on her tongue, and she smiled. A queen. Her strange gift, the one she had been forced to keep secret all her life, was unique. Because there could only be one queen.

Sanura sat up, scanning her surroundings. Slowly, the night came back to her, and she remembered where she was and what she'd done. She glanced at the bare patch of earth beside her and her stomach hollowed. She had fallen asleep in the arms of her malevolent angel, the creature who had killed for her and ravished her body. Ba'al had claimed her, and she knew in her very soul it was a claiming that would follow her even beyond death.

Sanura climbed to her feet, cataloging the myriad of aches and pains she had sustained from their lovemaking. He was a generous lover if not a gentle one. As she tugged her robe tightly around herself, she moved down the narrow path, her mind replaying their night over and over again. His mouth on every inch of her body. His firm grip as he guided her down atop him and brought her pleasure like she'd never known.

She smiled, touching her lips. After their lovemaking, he'd wrapped her in his arms and hummed softly as she closed her eyes and drifted into a dream, cocooned by his warmth.

Waking alone had unsettled her, but angels didn't sleep—he'd told her the night before. Surely, the King of the Dead had more important things to do than lie with his mortal lover while she slept.

She wrapped her arms around herself as she reached the Gavras home and slipped through its arched doorframe. A chill stole over her as she stepped inside.

"Where have you been?" Lysander stepped out of the kitchen, arms folded over his chest. His dark gaze was nothing like the jovial face that had greeted her so many times before; it was far too similar to the man who had nearly been her demise.

The bite of those words brought her last visit to Ba'al crashing to the forefront of her mind and her stomach churned. Sanura pressed a hand into the wall, struggling to hold back the bile rising in her throat.

Lysander's brooding mask broke as he lunged forward, sliding an arm under hers. "Sanura. What's wrong? Are you injured?"

"I," she inhaled sharply. "I." Her lungs constricted painfully as she tried and failed to get her breathing under control.

"Hey. Come sit down. Breathe."

Lysander ushered her to a cushion in the dining room, and she collapsed onto it, squeezing her eyes shut.

Sanura's breathing slowed in Lysander's calming presence, her heart finding a steady rhythm.

She opened her eyes, meeting his worried gaze. "I couldn't... be here last night. Had to get some air."

His face softened, and he smiled, reaching up to pull a stray branch from her tangled curls. "Did you wrestle a bush for a place to sleep?" His lips parted in a grin.

Sanura winced. "I wasn't ready to be... here."

The smile fell from Lysander's face, and he tucked a strand of hair behind her ear. "He can never hurt you again."

His words were more comforting than he knew, but it wasn't the kind man sitting beside her that soothed her fear; it was the angel who had righted a wrong—who had stolen her heart—and rescued her from a monster.

CHAPTER 21

Sanura

Sanura sank into steaming water, groaning as her sore muscles unwound. Her body ached in more places than she could count, but all were a reminder of Ba'al's lovemaking, each bringing forth a memory of his touch.

Agetha bustled into the room, pouring jasmine oil in beside her. She set a jug down and dropped to her knees. "Tip your head back, Lady. I will wash your hair."

Sanura obliged, staring up at the thickly thatched ceiling. Warm, scented water cascaded over her scalp, sending goosebumps rippling across her bruised skin. As Agetha massaged strong fingers into her skull, Sanura sighed, closing her eyes and sinking deeper into the tub.

A small gasp made her blink, and she twisted to face the housekeeper. Agetha dropped her gaze to the floor.

"What is it, Agetha?"

The woman shook her head, refusing to meet Sanura's eyes.

She shuddered, watching her carefully neutral, downcast features. "Agetha, I won't harm you. Tell me."

The woman's eyes lifted, meeting hers. "Your neck, Lady."

She touched the tender skin where Ba'al had sunk his teeth. "Bring me a mirror?"

Agetha nodded, rising to her feet, and raced from the room, returning with a small hand mirror and handing it to Sanura.

Sanura turned her head, glancing sideways at her reflection, and whimpered. She had felt her skin knitting together when he ran his tongue over it and had expected only bruising. Instead, a red raised circle was bisected by a five-pointed star. It looked more like a brand than a bite. She touched the mark with the pad of her finger, still tender but not bleeding. In the haze of lust-filled emotions the night before, she'd thought he bit her, but had he burned her?

"Agetha. You cannot tell anyone about this. Do you understand?"

The housekeeper's eyes were wide, but she nodded, knuckles going white around the jar she'd retrieved from the floor.

Sanura narrowed her eyes. "It would be very bad for you if you did."

The woman's grip tightened on the jar, and she nodded again.

"Knock, knock."

Sanura's gaze moved from the housekeeper to the door.

Helena stepped through, a bright smile painted across her shimmering golden face. Her face paint was heavily done, and Sanura suspected she'd have worn it this way long ago if not for fear of her father.

"You've been in this tub for ages, Cousin. Get dressed so we can go to market and choose new fabrics for the harvest festival."

Agetha ducked past Helena, escaping before Sanura could say more. It was a problem she would have to deal with later.

Sanura draped wet strands of hair over the mark, eyeing her cousin as she danced around her bath, humming to herself.

"I'm going to bring Aniel." Helena stopped spinning and faced her. "Don't give me that look. I will ask Lysander to speak with Erasmos. He'll explain it to him. Besides, I doubt Erasmos wants to honor the arrangement now that Father's gone." She seemed to realize the words were in poor taste a moment after they left her mouth, and her cheeks darkened.

Sanura sat up. "Would you hand me a towel?"

Helena turned, relief ghosting over her face before she twisted.

Sanura stood and stepped out of the tub, taking care to leave her hair in place.

Helena wrapped the towel around her and moved to the door. "Be quick, Cousin. I want to get something nice for tomorrow night." She disappeared out the door, leaving Sanura to drip onto the stone in silence.

Sanura trailed Helena through the market, and Aesop, as usual, darted between them, moving with the energy of a young boy. He seemed to know every street vendor and merchant, and all gave him a kind smile.

"You're looking very fine this evening."

Sanura spun to face the familiar voice. "Menelaos, right?"

He smiled, stepping up beside her. "I'm not sure if I should be offended that you had to guess my name."

Heat crept up Sanura's neck. "I apologize. I have had a great deal on my mind."

His playful smile fell. "It's I who should apologize. I was very sorry to hear of Antyamos's passing. I hope it won't stop you from attending tomorrow's festival."

"We wouldn't miss it," Lysander said, startling Sanura as he stopped beside her and settled a hand on her lower back.

Menelaos glanced between the pair, another smile creeping onto his face. "Will you be going with Lysander as your escort, then?"

"No, I..." Sanura started at the exact moment Lysander said:

"Yes."

She peered at him and stepped out of his reach. "I am Matron Leontia's guest and will be attending under her supervision."

Menelaos's grin stretched wider, and he chuckled. "Well then, I hope you'll save me a dance. I would love to teach you some of my favorites."

"She won't need—"

"That would be lovely," Sanura said, cutting Lysander off. She gave him a pointed look, and his brows dipped. For a moment, Sanura thought she had caught another glimpse of Antyamos in that look, but it was gone, and she wasn't entirely sure it had ever been there.

"What are you all doing holding my cousin back from the silk merchants?" Helena asked, approaching their group and grabbing Sanura's arm. Sanura let her tug her away, glad to escape the two men. "Menelaos exists to torment Lysander," Helena whispered conspiratorially into Sanura's ear as she pulled her past row after row of carts and tables laden with goods. "He's harmless, though. I think he does it to gain my brother's attention." She raised her eyebrows in a mock surprise, and Sanura darted a glance around.

"Don't say such things. Someone could overhear."

Helena let out a tinkling laugh. "This is Athens, Cousin. Men here are not chastised for their diversions."

Sanura's head spun as she glanced around the street, taking everyone in with fresh eyes. Her gaze lingered on a pair who stood abnormally close, drawing in a sharp breath when one of the men ran a finger down the other's arm and leaned in to whisper in his ear. As Helena had said, no one gave them a second look. In her village, those men would have been rolled in blankets and burned. What a strange and modern city she found herself in.

They stopped beside a table, sprawling with bright fabrics of every shade. Sanura ran her fingers over a dark tunic that reminded her of Ba'al's robes. Even the texture was similar.

"What is this material called?" she asked the merchant.

"That is velvet, Lady. All the way from Phoenicia."

A memory flashed through Sanura's mind of her hands tracing the outline of Ba'al's arousal and desire pooled low in her belly.

"Whoa, Cousin.

Sanura glanced up, heat creeping onto her cheeks, and she snatched her hand back as though it had been burned.

"If you like it that much, we'll get it but don't wear it around Lysander. He won't be able to control himself."

Sanura must have looked as bewildered as she felt because Helena laughed and wrapped an arm around her. To the vendor, she said, "We'll have some of this fabric, please." To Sanura, she said, "I can smell your desire. Nephilim gift. Gotta love it. Can't you smell people's emotions?"

She could, but she had always thought it was a gift uniquely hers.

CHAPTER 22

Sanura

Helena dumped her pile of fabrics into one of the house staff's waiting arms. "We'll need gowns for tomorrow, Irene. Sanura, give her your materials."

Sanura stepped through the arched doorway into their courtyard and dipped her chin. "Please, Irene, lead the way, and I will bring my fabric."

Helena rolled her eyes and swept up the stairs.

"I'll carry them," Lysander offered, holding out his arms.

"Brother. You will not."

Lysander stiffened, and Sanura whirled around to find a man in his middle years standing near the fountain.

He crossed the courtyard in four long strides and stopped in front of Lysander. "What do you mean by offering to do the work of the staff for them?"

Lysander scowled, but he didn't contradict the other man.

"You must be Sanura," he said to her. "Hand your things to Irene and meet me in the breakfast room. We have not yet been introduced." Without waiting for a reply, the man turned and marched through the open archway to their right.

Sanura wrinkled her brow, but Lysander shook his head, quickly following him.

Irene held up her already heavily laden arms, and Sanura settled her few new pieces on the others, looking apologetic. Irene darted away, disappearing into another room. Sanura turned reluctantly and followed them both into the breakfast room.

Lysander sat sullenly, and the other man sat at the head of the table, back straight, with small eyes narrowly observing everything around him.

"Come in. Let me see you."

Sanura's veins iced, but she moved swiftly to stand before him. He didn't rise from his chair or hold out a hand; she made no move to show deference.

"My father's arrangement with my aunt will stand," he began. "But know this. I am not a man for games or women who sully our family name. Put one toe out of line, and you will be on the next boat back to your hovel."

Hearing no question in his words, Sanura said nothing.

He stood abruptly, raising his hand.

Lysander shot to his feet, coming around the table. "Don't touch her, Georgios."

The man, Georgios, laughed—a terrifying sound, full of malice. "Mother said you were attached to her." His hand fell as he turned to face his younger brother. "Un-attach yourself. You are sworn to Phoebe. Or have you forgotten?"

Something uncomfortable simmered in Sanura's chest. She shouldn't care if he had a betrothed, considering her heart was already spoken for, but the words stung.

"I have agreed to nothing," Lysander spat.

"I am head of this house. I do not need your consent."

Lysander squared his shoulders, narrowing his eyes on his brother. He was taller, but Georgios was broader. Sanura had no doubt who would win in a fight between the two.

"My son!" Leontia swept into the room just in time, as she so often was, and Georgios's entire demeanor changed. The rage bubbling around them abated, and both sons turned their attention to their mother. Sanura was reminded again of the power this woman wielded. "Give me a hug, my beautiful boy."

She wrapped her arms around him, and he melted into her embrace. "Mother. We have guests. Please."

Even as he said the words, he leaned against her much smaller frame.

Leontia released her son, patting his cheek. "Nonsense. Sanura is family, and we will treat her as one of us."

Mother and sons continued speaking, chatting animatedly, but Sanura heard none of it. A warmth buzzed inside her, stretching along her limbs all the way to her fingertips and down to her toes. In her head, a fuzzy elation numbed her senses. She had felt nothing like it before.

Belonging.

When Georgios had settled into his seat and Lysander had grudgingly accepted his mother's placating words, Sanura slipped into her room and disrobed quickly. She lifted the trunk at the end of her bed and nearly doubled over at the smell.

She slammed it closed and reached for the robe resting on the chair in the corner, wrapping it around herself before sinking onto the bed. How had the house staff not found it yet? True, her senses were heightened compared with humans, but death never smelled so putrid. Something festered in the dead skin of Antyamos's flesh. If only she knew the name of the creature who had delivered it so that he may take it away.

"Ba'al," she whispered, hoping he would hear her call.

In her room, all was still and silent. Then she felt it: the insidious darkness creeping along the walls, sliding between shadows.

"Come out," she demanded.

A dark creature slithered over floorboards, solidifying at the center of her room and bowing before standing, towering above her.

She studied it. Where the first creature who had visited her had vaguely resembled a man, this one was akin to a giant scorpion. Muscles rippled down its torso where arms protruded, and a long tail whipped angrily from side to side at its back.

"Where is your king?"

The creature tilted its head. "Apologies, my queen. The king is detained and sends me in his stead."

Her chest buzzed in that same confident way it had when Ba'al had called her a queen. She stood a little taller. "There's a hand in my chest. I need you to get rid of it."

The creature bowed again. "I would, my queen, but it was a gift from my king. He wishes you to keep it."

Sanura huffed a frustrated breath. Her station didn't supersede his authority, it seemed. "I cannot keep it..." She paused. "What is your name?"

"Mazikin, my queen."

"Mazikin, please tell your king that it will mean my death if anyone finds it." Mazikin bowed one final time, disappearing.

Sanura paced the room. She had no way of knowing how long it would be before she heard from him, but with a mark on her neck and a rotting hand in her chest, it was only a matter of time before trouble found her.

Sanura exhaled through her mouth, trying not to gag on the smell. She should have taken Helena up on her offer to show her the best way in and out without detection. It hadn't seemed like she'd need that skill when the man whose hand she carried—wrapped in her nightgown—had died, but with Georgios in residence, perhaps one tyrant had been replaced by another.

She reached the cemetery and set her nightgown down, searching for a rock with a sharp tip. Spying one, she pried it from the soft dirt and dug.

When she had made a hole deep enough that dogs wouldn't dig it up, she shook out her nightgown and dropped the hand into the hole. Quickly filling it in, she stamped the earth until it was packed and began digging another hole several paces away. On the unlikely chance someone found the hand or the nightgown, they would not find the two together.

"What in Zeus's name are you doing?"

Sanura screamed, jumping so high she could have twisted an ankle. "Lysander? Are you trying to scare me to death?"

He stepped out of the darkness, peering around at the empty cemetery. "I have to admit, I thought you were meeting a lover when I saw you sneaking out." A dimple appeared on his cheek as he grinned. "But what are you doing digging holes in the middle of the night?"

Sanura reached down, shaking open her nightgown. "I was burying this."

Lysander's smile fell, and he stepped closer. "Whose blood is that?"

"Mine," she lied. "From the night it happened."

Lysander went impossibly pale as he reached for it, holding it up. Soaked in Antyamos's dark blood, it painted a gruesome picture.

It was a risk. He'd been there that night, after all. He'd seen her when she passed out and may have even known what happened to the clothing she'd worn, but she was hoping against hope that the house staff had discarded that nightgown and he'd had no involvement in it.

"I'm so sorry, Sanura. I should have been there." He fell to his knees, crumpling the nightgown in his fist, looking up at her with so much sorrow and regret that she almost felt bad for lying to him. "I should have stopped him sooner."

"It's not your fault. You didn't make him a wicked man." She sank to the ground beside him and rested a hand atop his. "And when it mattered, you were there." Their eyes met, and a tear slipped down his cheek. He nodded, letting her take the nightgown. "Help me bury it?"

She handed him the rock, and he speared the ground viciously, making a hole far too deep for her small bit of cloth. When it was done, they stood together, staring down at the packed earth. His hand found hers, and he laced them together.

The trembling in her fingers wasn't forced as she fought with everything she had to hold back the desire to call the thing begging her to release it from the confines of its new prison. She gripped Lysander's hand tightly, tugging him away from the cemetery and the growing cacophony of voices pleading with her.

When they reached the arched doorway outside the Gavras home, Lysander stopped, letting her hand fall. He cupped her face in his palms and leaned in, pressing his mouth to hers.

Sanura stumbled backward.

Lysander released her, looking stricken. "I'm so sorry. I didn't mean... I thought—"

"You are spoken for Lysander," Sanura said, steeling herself. Do you think it appropriate to kiss one woman, knowing you will wed another?"

His horrified gaze morphed into one of anger. "My brother doesn't speak for me. I won't marry her. He can't force me."

Sanura took a step back. "Perhaps you should settle matters before making any more advances."

Lysander opened his mouth, but she raced past him, through the courtyard, up the stairs, and into her room. Closing the door, she leaned against it and slid to the floor, wrapping her hands around her knees. Too many things could have gone wrong tonight, but the hand was gone, and she'd put some distance between herself and Lysander. It would make things easier when she told him the truth.

She exhaled a long, weary sigh and inched up the door.

Her chest spasmed a moment before he spoke.

"My love, why did you refuse my gift?"

CHAPTER 23

Sanura

Sanura crossed her arms over her chest. She was in no mood for more quarrelsome men this night. "Are you hoping I die so I may join you in your realm? Is that why you left a present that could get me killed?" She pushed off the wall, striding forward.

Ba'al appeared in the room, making no more pretense of being a man. Tonight, he wore a dark crown, wispy and incorporeal but very real. His sapphire eyes were inhumanly bright as he watched her stalk toward him.

She stopped before him and stared up. "Well? Is that your aim?"

His arms, dark and insubstantial, solidified as he wrapped them around her.

She was stiff in his arms before the hum of contentment in her chest calmed her, and she melted against him.

He ran light fingers down her back, tickling her skin through thin fabric, and leaned his cheek against hers. "Never, my love. I gave you a present, and I had hoped it would be useful to you."

"What would I need a hand for?"

His fingers inched up her spine, finding the nape of her neck, and he wrapped them in her hair. Pulling her head back, he tipped her face up and brushed his lips against hers.

Her eyes closed as some of the day's tension bled away. She drank him in, mouth moving on his, lips parting. Ba'al swept his tongue over hers, stroking languorously.

She moaned.

When they parted, he whispered against her mouth, "You command all dead things, do you not, my love?"

Sanura's eyes flew open, and she stared up at him, still trapped in his tight grip. "A hand?"

"I can think of many uses for a hand." His lips curled up.

"Sanura?"

Sanura caught herself before she fell as the man in her arms evaporated and her door opened.

Helena was standing in her doorway, staring at her strangely, and a cold stone settled in her stomach. How much had Helena seen? What did Ba'al look like to her in his inhuman form?

She turned ungracefully and flopped onto her bed, yawning loudly. "Yes?"

"Are you... okay?"

Sanura gave her a puzzled look. "Yes?"

"Were you... talking to someone?"

She quirked her lips in what she hoped was a sheepish grin. "I was practicing dancing. For tomorrow."

Helena's confusion fell away as she smiled, stepping inside. "Are you excited? I can't wait! I could teach you?"

"I've been practicing for quite a while." Sanura yawned again for emphasis.

Helena's smile fell, but she nodded.

She crossed the room and sank onto Sanura's bed beside her. "I looked for Lysander tonight. I was going to ask him to talk to Erasmos, but I couldn't find him anywhere." She rolled onto her back, staring up at Sanura's ceiling. "It's unfair how men get to go about at all hours, doing anything they please, but we are stuck indoors without a chaperone."

Sanura rolled over, staring up. "What might it be like to be a man?"

Helena glanced sideways at her. "We could do whatever we want. Go anywhere, choose a profession if we wanted. We could marry whom we choose." Her cheeks darkened, and the air thickened with a melancholy Sanura understood. "But we'd have those awful bulges under our tunics."

They both burst into a fit of giggles, clearing the oppressive sadness, and Helena slid off the bed. "I hope things work out." She bit her lip, looking at Sanura. "And for you and Lysander, too. He really likes you."

Helena left the room. Sanura watched her go silently. Perhaps it was better to let Helena think she returned his feelings. But her gut twisted in guilt, thinking for a moment what it might be like to truly take another person into her confidence.

She climbed under her blankets, closing her eyes. As she drifted to sleep, she imagined a world where she could do anything she liked and other people could be trusted.

CHAPTER 24

Sanura

Sanura flew up in her bed. Something had woken her. A loud crash sounded downstairs, and she scrambled up and raced from her room. At the bottom of the stairs, Helena's screeching reached her long before arriving at the arched breakfast room door.

"I won't. I won't! Mother, tell him!"

Leontia lifted a hand toward Helena, who was red-cheeked, black lines trailing down her face.

Helena turned red eyes on her oldest brother and leveled him with a glare that could have melted ice. "You aren't Father, and you're not in charge of me. You'll have to stake my palms to the altar if you want me to meet him in the temple because I. Won't. Do it!" She stormed past Sanura, out of the room, and through the courtyard.

"Aesop. Please follow your sister and ensure she does not cause trouble." Leontia gave her youngest son a nod, and he dashed out of a corner Sanura hadn't seen him hiding in.

Sanura's gaze darted between Georgios and Leontia, her brow wrinkling.

"Good morning, Dear. Please, come and sit. Break your fast with me." Leontia sat gracefully, but Georgios stomped away, saying nothing to either of them. "My two headstrong children," Leontia said, giving Sanura a pained smile.

Sanura sat, reaching for a bunch of grapes and slices of melon and setting them on her plate.

"It seems the wedding is not canceled," Leontia said after a long pause.

Sanura nodded, staring down at her plate. They sat in silence for a time, each lost in their own thoughts.

Helena raced by, sobbing loudly and shouting at Aesop to stop following her.

Sanura glanced at the door. "May I be excused, Matron?"

Leontia appraised her. "You know my son will never approve your marriage to Lysander."

Sanura started, looking up. "I did not... That is..."

"Though I think that might be a blessing?"

Sanura met her hazel-eyed gaze and stood, wrapping her arms across her chest. When Leontia nodded, she left the room.

At the top of the stairs, Helena's loud weeping drew her to her cousin's door. She knocked softly.

"Go away!"

"It's Sanura."

There was silence before a loud sniffle. "Come in."

Sanura cracked the door open and stepped inside. Helena was stretched out across her bed, head buried in her pillow. She sat beside her cousin and laid a hand on her back.

Helena heaved a great sigh and rolled over, staring up at her. "My life is ruined." Sanura bit the inside of her cheek to keep from laughing at her cousin's dramatic tone. Helena sat up. "I won't marry him. I'll kill myself first."

"Cousin. You're not wed yet. There's still time to change his mind," Sanura said. "What if you could persuade Erasmos to back out?"

Helena's puffy eyes brightened. "Do you think?" She stood. "Yes! Sanura, you're brilliant!" She raced from the room, leaving Sanura sitting on her bed.

Sanura went into her own room and found a shimmering golden gown laid out on her bed. She'd let Helena convince her to have something made for the festival after her cousin had insisted no one wore such dark, drab colors to a party. Helena had droned on about the lights and the color of the wheat long enough that Sanura had given in, if only to end the discussion. It was a beautiful gown, even if it wasn't her style, and she held it up to herself. She hummed softly, stripped out of her clothes, and slid the fabric on. It was so thin her skin pebbled through the material, and the dark skin around her nipples was visible through sheer fabric.

The door to her room burst open. Helena swept in, looking every bit a goddess.

Sanura turned toward her. "I can't wear this. It's indecent!"

Helena grabbed her fingers, spinning her in a circle. Helena's own sheer golden gown showed off her pink buds, too, and only the long belt, strung with golden tassels, covered the apex of her thighs.

"Nonsense. You are Persephone, a goddess renowned for a beauty so devastating it trapped even Hades. Here, I brought you a belt." Helena strung a golden rope around Sanura's hips, fastening it over her navel so it covered her dark curls visible through the fabric. "There, you see? Now, you only need some shimmer for your arms, and you will be magnificent."

Sanura's mouth flattened into a line. "I cannot leave the house in this, Helena."

Helena produced a pot from a pocket. "Hold still. Just a bit of dust here." She applied the dust to Sanura's shoulders. "And here." She ran a finger down each arm. "There." She stood back, admiring her work. "A goddess."

Sanura opened her mouth to protest, but Lysander stepped into the doorway, and words died on her tongue. The desire rushing off him smothered the air in the room, making it hard to breathe. He held himself rigidly in the frame, every muscle taught.

Helena's ruby-painted lips split into a wide grin. "Lye, you'll escort Sanura tonight, won't you?"

Sanura's gaze met his, and she swallowed.

He had said nothing, hadn't moved, and it looked as though to do so might be too much of a struggle for him.

Helena rolled her eyes at her brother. "She isn't a meal Lysander. Never mind. Come on, Cousin. We'll be each other's escorts." Her cousin grabbed her hand and tugged her toward the door. When they reached it, Lysander's arm shot up, barring their path.

His molars ground together before a single word slipped out. "No."

A thrill of fear raced down Sanura's spine. It was there again: the barely contained rage Antyamos had never successfully leashed. It lived in Lysander, though he was fighting it.

"I'm just going to change into something—"

"No," Lysander said again, but he had wrestled some of his composure back into place. "You look stunning, Sanura. Please, let me escort you." The hand he'd propped against the door to bar their path came down, and he held it out to her.

The room was cooler, some of Lysander's overwhelming yearning receding as he wrestled his emotions under control.

"Maybe you should have worn the velvet," Helena called over her shoulder as she slipped past Lysander, leaving them alone.

Did Helena believe she was doing her a favor? Had she truly misread her feelings so greatly?

"Shall we?" Lysander gave her a toothy grin that resembled a hungry wolf.

Sanura placed her hand in his, hiding her grimace at the slickness of his palm.

They left the house, Aesop trailing them all silently. Georgios wasn't with them, but neither was Erasmos. Leontia had left earlier to meet with their coven before the event began. That left the four of them to travel the path alone.

"I'm sorry about before," Lysander said, leaning down, and she could have sworn he smelled her hair. "I'm really nervous tonight."

"It's okay. This dress was a poor choice."

"No," Lysander choked on the word. "I've seen no one look so beautiful... as you do."

She grimaced again, wishing she could tug her hand from his. She'd let this go on too long and feared it might be too late. There was a side of him he tried to hide, an intense side that, given the correct set of circumstances, could prove dangerous.

For her.

Sanura gasped as she took in a transformed market. Lanterns were strung along each path in a crisscrossing pattern, lighting a newly cleared space at the center of a circle of nighttime vendor tables. Every stall was filled with steaming platters of roasted chicken, seasoned vegetables, bowls of jams and bread, and jugs of ale and wine. At the far end of a wide circle, three men played instruments, the tune carried as if by magic. Perhaps it was. Sanura spied several of her sisters, including Pythia, standing together, looking smug.

When she tipped her head back, staring up at the twinkling lanterns overhead, she could swear some were held by nothing at all. Even the light breeze carrying spices on the air seemed contrived, but she would not have changed a thing. Truly, this must be what magic was meant for.

Lysander's fingers squeezed around hers, bringing her back to the present. "Dance with me?"

Her lips drooped. For a moment, she was brave. For an instant, caught in the magic of this place, she believed she could be honest. "Lysander, I—" A wicked gleam flashed in his eyes, and she remembered herself. "Would love to."

His smile returned, though his grip had grown impossibly tight, and he led her into a group of swinging revelers. Sanura glanced around nervously, but his hand landed on the small of her back, and all her attention zeroed in on the crawling sensation of his fingers rubbing circles on her bare skin. The skin Ba'al had held. The skin he had pressed his mouth to and claimed.

Her stomach hollowed out as Lysander pulled her into a dance she was helpless to escape, spinning and spinning and spinning.

Laughter grew, and the music became cacophonous. Soon, the world was buzzing, a deafening roar in her ears. She tugged uselessly against his grip, but in the false light, his smile was a leer as the planes and hollows of his face were cast in shadow. When she whirled again, something terrifying was painted there.

"Lysander," she breathed. The merriment and revelry drowned her voice as he twirled her again and again. Her vision swam, and whispers from all the dead things around them called her.

"Sanura. Sanura, find me. Free me. Save me." They were an endless chant, shouting to be heard over stomping feet and clanking clay pots, over the strumming of strings against calloused fingers, and the clapping of palms.

"Sanura, see me. Free me. Raise me," a darker voice called to her. "Raise me. Raise me. Raise me."

She ripped her hand from Lysander's grasp, dropped to her knees, and covered her ears.

"No. Please. Stop," she begged, but none of it drowned the voices in her head.

The loudest, a man newly dead, desperately angry for his foul end. "Sanura. Raise me."

"Noooo!" she screamed, shooting her hands out to her sides.

Lysander sunk to his knees beside her but was thrown back when a shock wave blasted from her palms.

In the blissful silence, Sanura looked up, gaping in horror. All around her, the world was still. No one moved. She stood unsteadily and turned in a slow circle.

Cups had clattered to the ground and shattered, plates of food were covered in dust and dirt, and every person lay at an odd angle.

"No. No." She kept turning as if the image would change, but every spin was the same gruesome scene. "What have I done?" She brought a hand to her mouth, covering the sob that threatened to escape.

"Sanura?" Ba'al appeared, and she rushed forward, wrapping her arms around him. "Shhh. It's okay. It's okay."

"It's not okay. I killed them. All of them."

"No, my love. They aren't dead."

Sanura released him, looking up. "What?"

"Feel them. You would know if they were dead."

She swallowed, wiping the tears from her cheeks, and stepped back, opening up the senses she had slammed closed when the shockwave tore through her. He was right. They were unconscious, but they did not belong to her. Not yet.

She loosed a sigh. "I thought..."

Ba'al wrapped his arms around her once more. "They live."

She nodded.

A gasp from the other side of the market made Sanura look up. Ba'al evaporated in her arms, and when the dark smoke cleared, Helena was standing beside a vendor's cart, her mouth hanging open.

When her eyes locked with Sanura's, she rushed forward, throwing her arms around her. "What happened? I went to see Aniel, just for a moment, and when I returned..." She leaned back, looking Sanura over. "Were you not here either?"

Sanura shook her head, not trusting herself to speak the lie.

Helena pulled her in for another hug.

"Mother," she cried, releasing Sanura and racing to Leontia.

The matron sat up, holding a hand to her head, groaning. "Daughter?"

"Mother," Helena sobbed, falling to her knees and hugging her.

Motion behind a table caught Sanura's eye, and she moved toward it. A small sandy-haired boy darted from behind the cart and raced for his mother, tucking himself inside Helena's arms.

Around her, others were struggling to sit up, touching their heads and moaning.

Sanura searched the darkness, but Ba'al was gone. She moved to Lysander's side and rested a hand against his cool cheek. He wasn't moving, and when she closed her eyes, she felt it: the tug of a soul, asking her to guide it. A single tear rolled down her cheek. She had done this to him.

No matter how she'd feared him the last few days, he didn't deserve it.

She laid her head on his chest. "I'm so sorry. Please, Lysander, don't go. Wake and return to us."

She jumped, stumbling backward when his lids flew open, and he sat up—too fast. His gaze shot around, landing on her. His eyes had changed, and so had his energy. When he looked at her, they gleamed golden in the lantern light. Like hers.

Chapter 25

Sanura

Helena dropped to her knees beside Lysander and threw her arms around him. "Lye! You're okay!"

He sat motionless, staring at Sanura.

Sanura shivered as terror settled into her bones. He had been dead. There was no doubt. But somehow, she had brought him back. She felt the soul lingering in his body that didn't belong there and knew it was her doing.

"Lye?" Helena shook him, trying to wake him from his stupor, but Sanura feared there would be no returning from the daze he lived in now. Helena's gaze followed her brother's to Sanura, and she rose slowly. "Sanura, help him. There's something wrong with him."

Sanura leaned forward, touching his cheek. "Lysander. Can you hear me?"

"Yes." His voice was flat.

"Are you well? Can you stand?"

He stood too fast for a human, and Helena glanced around nervously. The humans were still struggling to stand or pick up broken plates and jugs, and no one was paying them any mind.

Sanura climbed to her feet. "Come with us, Lysander, but act human." Lysander stepped forward, and Helena gave Sanura a worried glance. "Go get your mother and Aesop. I'll bring him back to the house."

Helena nodded, racing back to Leontia and Aesop.

When they were gone, Sanura turned to Lysander and laced her fingers in his, trying to settle the thrum of nervous tension tearing through her. "Lysander, can you think for yourself in your new state?"

"I will do as my queen wishes."

Sanura swallowed. *Truly dead.* She tugged him with her, and they left the lighted space, moving up the stone path toward the Gavras home. He walked silently, matching her pace, his fingers remaining interlaced with hers. As they neared his home, trepidation stole over her. How would they ever believe this creature was still alive? Her gaze darted to him, and she frowned.

"Lysander, can you learn to act on your own so I don't have to remain with you at all times?"

He tugged them to a stop.

Sanura turned to face him. His unnatural eyes reminded her of Ba'al, but their color was gold, like hers. Not an angel of death or a dead human. Something new.

"What is it, Lysander?"

"I never want to leave your side, my queen."

"We cannot always be together."

He frowned, and her heart lightened. It was a human emotion. "If I think for myself, can we be together?"

"When it's proper." His brows furrowed. "And perhaps one day, more often than that."

Lysander's teeth flashed in the darkness, and he resumed walking.

"Lysander?" He glanced at her. "This will only work if no one knows what you are. You must convince everyone you're the same. Never tell them what has happened to you."

Sanura's gaze slid over him as they went. Although she couldn't imagine his mother not noticing the change in him, she wasn't likely to think him dead. Perhaps that would be enough. If Leontia had proved one thing, it was that she would overlook a lot to keep up the facade of a happy home.

Sanura slipped into her bed, groaning at the ache in her chest. It was as if some internal battery had been depleted when she used that burst of magic at the festival. Shuffling in the hall had her sitting up. The sound came again, and she hopped out of bed, throwing her door wide.

"What are you doing here?" she hissed.

Lysander stood just outside her door. "I don't want to be parted from my queen."

"Come in. Hurry." She ushered him inside and closed the door behind him. He stopped in the middle of her room. "I thought I was clear," she said. "You can't be here when it isn't proper."

He blinked at her, saying nothing.

"It isn't proper at night."

He crossed his arms over his chest. "My room is boring, and I'm not tired."

A small laugh escaped her. "Well, I am."

"Why is there a man in your room, my love?"

Sanura spun, lifting a hand to her temple. "You can't be here either, Ba'al."

"If the man can be here, I certainly can."

The growl in his voice made her toes curl, but she dropped her hand and glared at him. "You know very well he isn't a man any longer. I'm certain you feel it."

"Yes, I see," he said. "Not one of mine, though. Something new."

"So you don't know what he is?"

Ba'al shook his head, stalking closer and leaning in to inspect Lysander.

Lysander waved a hand in front of his face as if he were swatting a fly, and Ba'al backed up, eyes going wide.

A snort escaped Sanura, and both Ba'al and Lysander looked at her.

"What will you do with him?" Ba'al arched an eyebrow at her.

"I had hoped to return him to his family."

"This creature could never pass for a man," Ba'al said, continuing his inspection. "Does he eat?"

Sanura bit her lip. "I don't know."

Ba'al repeated the question to Lysander.

"I could eat," Lysander said in his strange monotone voice.

"Ah, but what do you crave?"

Lysander considered. "I would love a honey cake right now."

"Fascinating," Ba'al said loudly.

"Shhh!" Sanura rushed forward, pressing a finger to his lips. "I'm not allowed to have men in here." Ba'al nipped at her finger playfully, and a grin crept onto her lips. "Stop." She looked at Lysander, who was glowering at Ba'al.

"Did this human have feelings for you?"

"He was a Naphil."

Ba'al's brows shot up. "Was he? He doesn't like me very much."

"I want to test something," Sanura said, looking back at Lysander. Will you help me?"

Ba'al's mouth curled up. "Absolutely."

"Kiss my hand."

"As my love wishes." Ba'al lifted her hand to his lips, pressing a lingering kiss to her knuckles.

Her chest purred in response, and a blush crept onto her cheeks. She glanced at Lysander, whose eyes had narrowed, but he hadn't moved.

"Now, hurt me."

Ba'al frowned. "No."

"Nothing dangerous."

He raised a brow.

"What about a bite? A small one." His lips lifted, and she held out a hand pointing to a spot on her forearm.

Ba'al dipped his chin and lifted her wrist to his mouth. He bared his teeth, sinking them into her skin.

She hissed even as desire bloomed to life between her thighs.

Lysander appeared beside them and gripped Sanura's arm in an unnaturally firm hold, working to pry Ba'al's mouth off her.

Ba'al's sharp teeth lifted, and Lysander stepped back. Ba'al ran his tongue over the wound, movements unhurried, licking her blood clean. He pressed a kiss to her tender skin as his gaze moved slowly to Lysander. "You'll have to do better than that if you hope to best me, child."

Ice erupted along Lysander's palm, and two glistening spikes pierced her lover faster than Sanura could register.

Ba'al chuckled darkly, and the spikes melted, soaking his dark velvet tunic. A thin trail of golden blood followed, and Sanura watched in fascination as the holes closed. He grinned as he wrapped long fingers around Lysander's neck, nails lengthening into dark talons.

Lysander flailed wildly as he tried to tug Ba'al's sharp fingers free.

"Stop," Sanura ordered. "He was protecting me."

Ba'al released Lysander, eyeing him. Dark rings circled his throat, and three small punctures were quickly turning black.

Sanura stepped closer, frowning and touching one of the marks before she looked back at Ba'al. "Promise you won't hurt him again."

Noise outside Sanura's door made her freeze.

"Sanura, are you awake?" Helena asked from the other side of the door.

Sanura's eyes went wide, and she glanced between Lysander and Ba'al. "Help," she mouthed.

Ba'al's gaze narrowed, but he wrapped his arms around Lysander's waist, turning and diving out the window.

The creak of the door drowned out Lysander's muffled protests as Helena pushed into the room. She stared at Sanura standing in the middle of the room and looked around. "I swear, ever since you moved in, I feel as though I'm going mad. I hear men's voices in here every night."

Sanura lifted a shoulder.

Helena came in and paced around, peering into the darkened corners. She glanced back at Sanura and dropped down, looking under the bed. "Hmm." She stood, dusting her knees, and went to the window, leaning out. "Well, anyway, I just wanted to check on you after everything tonight."

Sanura nodded. "I'm okay."

"The thing is, Aesop thinks he saw something."

A stone settled in Sanura's stomach as Helena turned to face her again.

"He thinks he saw you throw out your hands and knock everyone down." She raised her chin. "But... air magic like that would take a lot of practice and power." She paced away from Sanura, then turned back to her. "Neither of which you have."

Sanura was frozen in place, working desperately to school her features into something resembling confusion rather than blind terror.

"You know kids. Wild imaginations." Helena laughed, moving to the door. "Okay, well... If you ever want to talk, let me know."

Her unspoken question hung in the air, but Sanura didn't trust herself to speak, so she only nodded again.

"Good night." Helena closed the door, and Sanura let out a great sigh of relief, sinking onto her bed.

She slid under her blankets and closed her eyes, taking calming breaths. Helena sounded skeptical of Aesop's story. No one would believe the words of a child when they were so farfetched. She inhaled again, more slowly, and exhaled. It may be time to have a chat with Aesop.

CHAPTER 26

Aesop

Aesop ducked under the cook's counter and ran a hand along its smooth surface until he touched cold clay. Fingers inching over the lip of the plate, he snatched a honey cake and stuffed it into his mouth. Feet shuffled by in every direction. Hurrying, he grabbed another cake.

"Aesop!"

He crammed it into his mouth and slid around the table, running out the door before the cook could catch him and swat his fingers.

In the middle of the courtyard, Aesop froze when Helena shouted from the top of the stairs. When he was sure she hadn't seen him, he dashed behind the fountain at the center and fished in his pocket for the copper bit he'd found that morning on the path.

He peeked a head over the edge of the fountain and made a wish that Sanura would leave so everything could go back to the way it was before she came. Before his father died, Lysander was changed, and her dark magic touched everyone at the party. Everyone except him and Helena. She'd been with her boyfriend again.

The coin sailed through the air and splashed into the second tier of the fountain. A good omen. He nodded to himself and dared another peek before racing across the courtyard to the bathing rooms.

His mother wasn't humming as she normally did when she bathed. Aesop pressed his back to the wall and glanced at the piece of glass above the sink, watching his mother's reflection.

She rubbed her temples, eyes closed, brows drawn low.

A dark five-pointed star was painted on her forehead, but it wasn't the kind of paint humans could see. It wasn't even the kind other witches could see. Only *he* could see it.

He saw the curses they put on one another with their tainted words and bad wishes. He saw the energy that leeched from them into everything and everyone around them, feeding the earth as the earth fed them. He saw what Helena's boyfriend truly was and what the man who followed Sanura was. He knew Lysander was no longer alive, even though the others didn't.

His mother tipped her head back and moaned softly. Her star was darker than the others. Somehow, she'd been affected by Sanura's magic more than the rest, all except Lysander.

Georgios hadn't been at the party. He was safe. So was Erasmos, so he could still marry Helena even though she was already mated to Aniel.

Aesop slipped into the room and watched his mother to be sure she wouldn't open her eyes. He stuffed his hand into his pocket, pulled out the buds of chamomile he'd gathered in the field beside their house, and rubbed them between his palms, letting the bits of broken flowers fall into her bath.

Its sweet honey apple fragrance wafted to his nose, and he breathed it in. He stayed a moment—smiling as the dark mark on her forehead faded—before darting out of the room. It wasn't a cure, but it would help with her headaches.

Listening for any sound of his siblings, Aesop skipped up the stairs to his sister's room and pressed the door open gently. He glanced around before slipping inside and crossing to her table, lifting a jar of gold powder she dusted on her arms with every day. Pulling a stalk of rosemary out of his other pocket, he stripped several needles off, dropping them in. He replaced the lid on the pot and backed out, closing the door gently.

"Hey!"

Aesop looked up, eyes going wide as Sanura stalked toward him. He stumbled back, shoulder blades pressing into the wall.

"I have been looking everywhere for you." She held out a hand with a honey cake on it. "Want one?"

He glanced down at the cake and backed up. He smelled no poison. Grabbing it, he quickly stuffed it into his mouth.

"Can we talk?"

He shook his head, chewing the sticky dessert.

"I promise I'm not mad at you. I just want to talk."

Her intentions weren't hostile at the moment. She wouldn't hurt him, but she was certainly capable of it. He wondered if she knew Lysander's blood was painted on her soul. Probably not. No one saw those things but him.

"Okay."

She beckoned him to follow her, and they went to a room at the end of the hall—not her room, which was good. He wouldn't have gone in there. Too much demon essence for his liking.

He followed her in and slid his hands into his pockets. He found the smooth stone Dina had given him to protect against false sight and rubbed his fingers over it, reassuring himself that he would know if her intentions toward him changed.

"Last night, something strange happened," she began.

Aesop swallowed, rolling the rock between his thumb and forefinger.

"But I don't think you saw what you think you did. I just wanted you to know the truth."

Lie.

"I was dancing with Lysander."

Truth.

"And I saw someone I thought I knew."

Lie.

"So I left the party to go to them, and by the time I realized they weren't who I thought they were, everyone had fainted. I rushed back to Lysander and checked to see if he was breathing. Luckily, he was."

All lies.

"So I'm not sure what you thought happened, but I promise you, I had nothing to do with it."

Her lies were so bitter on his tongue that they burned, making him wish he could gargle with salt to get the taste out of his mouth. The stone was growing warm as he rubbed it faster and faster, but his temper was rising too, and he hated her lies and everything she'd done to his family and his brother. "I know what you did to everyone. I won't let you take them. I'll keep them safe from you!" He pushed past her, rushing out the door.

"Aesop! Wait!"

114

He ran down the stairs, through the courtyard, under an archway, and into the street. He raced down the hill and through the market and kept running until he reached the temple and dropped to his knees at Dina's statue. Tears streamed down his cheeks, and he pulled her stone out of his pocket and closed his eyes.

"Please help us, Dina. She'll kill us all."

Featherlight fingers touched his shoulder, and his eyes flew open as the glowing, ethereal form of their patron angel landed on the marble floor. She knelt beside him.

Aesop threw his arms around Dina, and his tears soaked her pristine white tunic as she held him.

When his tears subsided, he looked up, meeting swirling iridescent eyes, and wiped his cheeks.

"Please send her away," he said. "Father died because of her, and now she's killed Lysander. Mother said you told her Sanura would be special, but she's not. She's evil."

Dina smiled, lifting Aesop in her arms so they were at eye level. "She isn't special because she's good, child. She is special because she will help us catch someone very bad. And when she does, we will rid the world of evil. Do you understand?"

Aesop nodded slowly. "And will any more of my family die for it?"

"I'm afraid so, little one. It is my family's burden to pay the price for the good of the world."

His vision blurred, and he swiped his eyes. "Please don't take Mother."

"I cannot tell you how it ends, and truly, I do not know, but this must be. Do you remember why I gave you true sight?"

He nodded. "To see the truth."

Dina smiled, reaching for the stone he had set beside her sculpture and handed it to him. "That's right, Aesop. You have the most important job of all my family. You must live so the tale is told and no one ever forgets what happened here."

CHAPTER 27

Sanura

Sanura's eyes blinked open, and she sighed. Her sleep had been as fitful as the previous three nights. Ba'al hadn't returned. Neither had Lysander.

Leontia paced at night, a silent phantom haunting their halls. When Antyamos died, she'd seemed much unaffected, but in Lysander's absence, dark circles rimmed her eyes, and her knuckles were white from ringing them.

Helena remained in her room until late into the day, only coming out for their evening meal. Georgios had taken up his father's position in government. Aesop, the ghost that he was, hadn't appeared since Sanura had tried to speak with him after the festival.

A light knock came at her door, and she sat up, rubbing her eyes. "Come in."

Agetha stepped in on silent feet, carrying three dark gowns. With all that had occurred these past days, Sanura had forgotten about Agetha's dangerous knowledge of her secret brand. The woman laid the gowns across Sanura's chest, not meeting her eyes.

"Thank you, Agetha."

She bobbed her head, looking at the floor as she made her quick escape, closing the door behind her. It seemed she had said nothing to anyone yet, but she was a loose end Sanura would need to tie up soon.

Tossing her blankets aside, she slid out of bed to inspect her new tunics. They were finer than anything she'd ever worn. As she ran a finger over crimson velvet, memories of her night with Ba'al resurfaced. She ached for his touch, but it wasn't safe to seek him out with Lysander missing and the house unsettled.

Her thoughts strayed to Aesop's strange words: *I know what you did to everyone, but I won't let you take them. I'll keep them safe from you!*

A dark sense of foreboding hung in the air, making her shiver. When the power building in Sanura had threatened to overwhelm her, the release had been involuntary, a desperate need to end the droning of the dead—of one dead man in particular. Somehow, for the first time, it had affected the living as well. And Lysander...

His soul clinging to his corpse had compelled her to act, to return the soul to the body lingering by will alone, but she wasn't sure how long it would last or what it meant for him. There was only one place she could go for answers. Only one she could ask who could not share her secrets with the living. *Tonight.*

Sanura pulled soft fabric over her shoulder and smiled to herself. The feel against her skin would be her constant reminder of him when he wasn't near. She moved down the stairs, stopping in the breakfast room to grab a pear. She bit into the buttery fruit, letting its rough granules roll over her tongue.

"That's a rather drab tunic for market."

Sanura started, looking up to find Georgios Gavras—the new head of their household—lounging in the room's corner.

As with their last encounter, he didn't rise, didn't demand she kiss his ring or show deference, but his dark eyes bored into her. Though he wasn't Naphil like the others, she sensed his magic.

"Do you go to meet my brother?" Her face must have shown her confusion because Georgios sat forward, observing her with the same too-keen stare his mother wielded. "When was the last time you saw Lysander?"

"Me?"

His mouth flattened into a thin line. "I see no others in the room with us."

"I... I think the night of the festival."

His brow dipped. "He has not come to your room?"

Sanura's cheeks flamed. It was a bold accusation—one that might cost Sanura her life. "No."

Georgios stood, crossing the room to stand in front of her. She looked up, meeting his hard eyes as he searched her face, cataloging some tell she hadn't hidden well enough.

"Have you not foisted yourself upon my brother in some desperate bid to better your station?"

Sanura's mouth fell open. "What?"

He crowded closer, leaning in to inspect her. "Your eyes are unique. What does Mother's coven say about them?"

She tore her gaze from his, looking down. She'd become too comfortable with this family. Had forgotten to safeguard her secrets.

Georgios lifted a hand, coiling a strand of Sanura's hair around a finger, and her stomach flipped. "This hair is unusual, too."

Sanura balled her fists at her sides, stilling her trembling fingers. This time, though, she did not quiver in fear but a barely suppressed rage. She had cowered to men like this all her life, showing deference and respect to those much weaker. And what had it gotten her? She'd nearly died at the hands of this man's father.

"Well? Speak when your better commands it."

Icy rage coursed through her veins, and she looked up, meeting his gaze. His eyes widened, and he took an involuntary step back.

"They say I'm powerful." She leaned closer, letting him see the storm brewing inside her. "They say I may be stronger than them all."

Georgios's eyes widened further, brows shooting into his hairline.

She stepped toward him, some of the ice chilling her veins leaching into her fingertips. It would be so easy to show this man just how powerful she was, to make him pay for every hateful thing he had said or done to those he considered beneath him. She uncurled a fist, lifting one hand.

"Good morning."

Leontia's voice cut through the haze of fury threatening to consume her, and she let her hand fall to her side. Water warmed at her fingertips and dripped to the floor.

Leontia moved into the room, linking an arm through Sanura's. "I've been looking for you, Sanura. We have a meeting with our sisters this morning."

Shaking herself from her savage thoughts, she nodded.

"Georgios, please go to the Acropolis today and ask Menelaos if he has seen Lysander. It is unlike him to stay away for so long. I fear for his safety."

Georgios schooled his features into neutrality, nodding. "I'm sure he's well, Mother, but I will ask."

She smiled, but it didn't reach her red-rimmed eyes.

Sanura's gut twisted. What if what she'd done to Lysander wasn't temporary? What if he was truly gone now? What if Ba'al had done something to him in retribution for his actions three nights before? Her lover had already shown how cruel he could be.

Leontia's arm tightened around Sanura's, and she glanced up. Had the matron somehow intuited her thoughts? Leontia gave her another sad smile, and she realized the woman leaned in for support rather than suspicion, so Sanura squeezed her arm back.

They reached the temple just before midday. Helena had been difficult to rouse and slower still to ready herself. As they rushed up the marble steps, Sanura wasn't entirely certain what they were late for. It wasn't the first of the week or the month, but perhaps this was another meeting she didn't know about. She was still learning what being a part of this coven meant.

Helena trailed them, her melancholy wilting the flora as she passed, but if she noticed how her mood affected the plant life, she didn't show it.

Leontia pressed the pattern on the stones Sanura believed she had finally worked out, and they moved swiftly down the dark stairs. As Sanura's sight adjusted to the soft orange glow suffusing the room, she took in her sisters circling the dais and atop it, a sacrificial lamb. They each held a bowl filled with its dark lifeblood and hummed softly.

Leontia and Helena rushed forward, picking up bowls, and took turns holding them at the base of the dais. Sanura followed, finding one remaining bowl, and lifted it. She glanced around, noting all the others were silver. Perhaps they had not had time to make one for her, but her stomach did another somersault as she lifted the dark pewter bowl and stepped up to the dais. Her palms were slick with sweat, and she gripped it tightly, steadying her trembling fingers.

She held up her bowl, prepared to accept the lifeblood when the humming stopped, and with it, the blood flowing from the dais. She turned stiffly, dread pooling in her belly.

Each of her sisters had drawn a vertical line of crimson on her forehead and bisected it by a horizontal one.

Sanura gripped her bowl, knuckles going white as she met each of their cold, condemning eyes. "What is this?" she breathed.

In the low light, their eyes gleamed with enough malice to send another spike of fear jolting through her. Sanura was powerful, but this many Nephilim against one? Her odds were bad.

Her gaze darted to Leontia, who watched her with more malice than the rest. Her mind raced through all their interactions, all the kindnesses the matron had shown her, and her heart sank. How many times had the bitterness coated her tongue when Leontia spoke, and she had dismissed it, wishing the words were true?

She turned her focus to Helena, the only member of their coven who didn't meet her eyes.

Finally, Sanura met Pythia's stare. Pythia, the girl who giggled over boys and dreamed of a love that would devour the world, looked more serious now than Sanura had ever seen.

"Undo what you have done to us. Return Lysander, and we will let you live."

CHAPTER 28

Sanura

Sanura swallowed, gaze darting back to Leontia. The matron's eyes were shining, hate-filled tears brimming along her lashes.

"I have done nothing to you," Sanura breathed.

"Where's Lysander?" Leontia shrieked, her composure crumbling.

"I swear, Matron, I don't know where he is."

Leontia dropped to her knees. Sanura rushed forward, but a blast of wind shoved her back. She hit the dais, and a crack sounded. She cried out, clutching her spasming back.

Helena helped Leontia to her feet, and they backed up, dipping into the shadows as the others closed in around her. Three women in the circle raised their hands, fire bursting to life in their palms.

A mirthless laugh spilled from Sanura's lips. "Have you decided my guilt, then?"

"We will let you live if you undo your curse and return Lysander," Pythia repeated.

Pain radiated down Sanura's leg, but she bit down on a whimper. She would not show weakness to these women. "Pythia, I swear to you, I do not know where he is."

"Aphrodite. Come forward." Helena stepped out of the shadows. "Tell us your truth."

Helena's gaze darted to Sanura, then back to the floor. "I was with... my lover... and when I returned to the festival, Sanura was embracing darkness." She looked up, gaze narrowing. "Then, before my eyes, the darkness vanished, and she was alone, standing in the middle of the dancefloor." Her voice hardened. "I ran to my mother to help her, and when I looked again, Sanura had her palms pressed against Lysander's chest." She glanced around the circle. "I thought I was seeing things. The darkness embracing her, the black magic seeping from her fingers when she laid her hands on Lysander, but..." She bit her lip. "My little brother saw it, too. He says..." She inhaled sharply. "He says we all bear her mark now."

"Helena. It's not true."

A collective gasp rose around the circle, and Pythia pinned Sanura with her dark stare. "We do not use our real names here."

A sweat trickled down Sanura's back, her breath coming in sharp bursts. She hadn't cursed them. She would know if she had. "Aphrodite," she began again. "I didn't hurt your brother, I swear. And I would never... I—"

"Aphrodite. Do you have anything else to share?" Pythia cut her off.

Helena's cheeks darkened. "Yes."

"Go ahead, Sister."

"I have a drawing of the mark on your foreheads," Helena continued. "The mark only my brother can see. I was told the giver will bear a physical brand to match it." She withdrew a scroll from her pocket, unrolling it, and held it up.

Sanura gripped her bowl, fighting the urge to bring a hand to her neck. How? How could Helena know about it?

Agetha.

The ice in her veins was building, expanding, and soon, it would need an outlet.

Helena rolled the scroll back up and slid it into her pocket.

Pythia returned her focus to Sanura. "Undress and prove to us the story is not true."

The bowl in Sanura's grip cracked, splitting down the center. It dropped to the floor, coated in a thick sheen of ice.

Several of the witches gasped. "Black magic," someone whispered, but Sanura couldn't see who in the low light.

She lifted her chin. "I don't need to prove myself to you. I passed your tests. I am one of you."

"You're nothing like us," Pythia seethed. "Remove our curse, or we will make you." She raised her hands, and branches erupted from the earth. They were wild, living things, thrashing under Pythia's hold, and they raced forward, a small branch lashing Sanura's cheek.

Dark blood welled up and ran in hot rivulets down her chin and neck, soaking into the crimson fabric along her collar. She threw up her hands, calling all the bits of dead bark resting beneath her feet and sending them spearing for the witches.

They cast an air shield, easily blocking her efforts, and three of the women lunged forward, shoving the wind at her hard enough to send her sprawling across the dais.

Sanura screamed as the last of the blood from the creature at the top of the dais soaked into her back. Quickly, she sat up and raised her hands again, but the Nephilim were faster, calling more roots and vines to them to tie her down. A ring of fire burst to life around her, flames rising higher and higher until they reached the ceiling above, the heat licking at her sides.

"If you're truly one of us, the flames won't burn you, right Persephone?" Pythia yelled over the roaring blaze.

Sick dread bubbled up in Sanura's chest as she wriggled in her restraints. If she could reach the ground, she could call on the dead to aid her, but her arms and legs were secured to the table, and each time she moved, they tightened. The flames dipped on some invisible wind, coming closer, and she squeezed her eyes against the searing heat radiating along her body. The hairs on her arms singed and blackened as flames reached for her, and her hair caught, sparking in a crimson fire.

"Stop!" she cried. "I didn't curse you, I swear!"

"Please, Persephone, tell us where Lysander is, and this will stop," Helena's pleading voice called over the fire.

Blistering, agonizing heat burned her scalp, and Sanura let out a blood-curdling cry as pain such as she'd never known tore through her.

"Stop!" Helena screamed. "Stop, you'll kill her!"

The flames around Sanura winked out, but the pain didn't recede. The roots pinning her in place were cutting into her skin, blood soaking them and mingling with the lamb's. Her heart pounded painfully in her chest, and the room tinged blue as the ice in her veins rushed to the surface. She threw back her head, screaming.

Spikes of ice tore from her hands, shooting into the dimly lit space, and a great shuddering rumble started beneath the dais. The pain had blocked it before, but she felt it now. It was coming. *He* was coming.

Her chest spasmed and swelled, and when the room went dark, the thing living inside her that somehow belonged to her lover burst with joy.

CHAPTER 29

Samael

In the absolute darkness, only he could see their horror—their horror—at realizing who had breached their sanctum. Their terror was a sweet symphony, drowned only by the sick fear radiating from the dais. From his soulmate.

"What have you done to her?" His words were laced with enough power that each Nephilim fell to their bellies, forced to bend under his wrath.

"Ba'al," his mate called, the sound of her broken voice sending a fresh bout of icy rage spearing through him.

They would pay for every scratch, every bruise. Ten times. One hundred times. They would scream until their throats bled, until they clawed their own eyes to escape the visions he poured into their minds. When they writhed in unending terror in his domain, they would know what true suffering was.

He wrapped poisoned talons in their Pythia's coiling black hair and wrenched her up. "Did you think you could harm my mate and survive it?"

Her screams echoed off the darkened walls, and she flailed wildly in his grip, some of her hair tearing free.

"Your screams are like a banshee," he groaned; delighting in her torment would be insufferable while she made those wild goat-like noises.

He tossed her to the ground, grinning as her ankle cracked sharply before she began howling again. Leaning down, he wedged his talons into her mouth, spearing the thick tongue reverberating between her teeth, and tore it free. She gurgled and choked on her blood, grabbing her throat before going blessedly silent.

"Ba'al," Sanura said weakly.

He moved to her side, slicing through the roots tying her down, and lifted her gently. Her body trembled violently, and he ran a finger along her blistered, burned cheek, hugging her to his chest.

Her scalp was blackened, thick ichor oozing from it, and the sight of all they had done to her intensified his rage. He would make them all pay. But first, Sanura needed his blood.

He sliced a vein along his arm, and golden liquid spilled free, dripping onto her lips. "Drink, my love. It will heal you."

Sanura's lips were blistered from the heat of their flames, and her teeth clattered together, but she opened her mouth and accepted his blood.

Her scalp scabbed over, peeling away quickly, and new hair sprouted and grew before his eyes. Bubbled, blackened skin along her arms and neck revived, leaving smooth skin where the burns had been.

She moaned, and her limbs ceased shaking.

Feeling better, my love?

She blinked up at him with new dark lashes. "Did you say something?" Her voice was still scratchy but healing.

I spoke in your mind.

Can I do it, too? she asked into his mind.

He chuckled, brushing her lengthening hair back from her face. Even after such a terrible ordeal, her mind was sharp and consumed with thoughts of him. *Of course. We are soulmates. Soulmates can speak to each other this way.*

A radiant smile broke over Sanura's freshly healed face and the half of his soul living within him, full to bursting with love for his other half, swelled. Perhaps he would bring her along to watch as he dreamed up torments to fill their eternity.

"Samael."

He looked up, eyes narrowing. "Sister."

Dina dropped to the ground, illuminating the room in her infuriatingly exalted glow. Raphael, Sariel, and Aniel landed behind her.

"What's this? An intervention?"

"Too long have you tarried on this plane," Dina said. "You have found your mate. Will you not take her and retire to your realm to leave the humans in peace?"

My love, I need a moment with my siblings. Go to our spot. I'll meet you there soon.

Sanura peered, wide-eyed, between her mate and the four glowing paragons before she nodded and slid out of his arms. She made a soft sound of pain as she moved, and he knew she felt the tug of their bond—the cruel, twisted gift their father had bestowed upon them as a reminder of their folly in creating the Nephilim.

The other Nephilim scrambled to their feet, darting away, several carrying their Pythia.

"What's this about, siblings?"

Raphael stepped forward, crossing his arms over his chest. "You think it unclear?"

Samael rolled his eyes. "I would hear it from anyone but the court jester. I beg you."

Raphael took another step, but Dina held up her hand. "Please, Samael, we only ask you to take your mate and go. You hold no dominion here. Why stay?"

"I enjoy the mortal plane. It holds many diversions for me."

Dina's mouth fell into a flat line. "Surely none so enticing as your other half."

"Have you missed that your coven failed to end her life?" He quirked a golden brow at his sister.

"A bit of poison would resolve that."

Samael barked a laugh. "As you did with your mate?"

"I did not. I could not."

Samael raised his hands in mock surrender. "Fair. Though I suppose it was too inconvenient for you to warn him against the dangers of uncooked meat."

Dina squared her shoulders, preparing to launch herself at him, but Aniel held her back. "Brother, the Nephilim are under our protection. Pythia is one of Raphael's, and you know Helena is my mate. You cannot harm them."

Samael's skin expanded as he grew, stretching toward the ceiling in the cavernous space. "Can't I? Who will stop me?"

The others stretched with him, filling the room.

"We will," Dina challenged.

Samael smirked. "Are we at war, then? I've been quite bored." He examined his nails, letting them lengthen once more into gleaming tips. "Nothing gives me pleasure like taking your wings."

The group pulled their silvery wings against their backs, some likely remembering a time or two when he'd done just that.

"I have a proposal," Aniel offered. "The coven will not harm your mate. When she reaches the end of her mortal life, she'll join you. In exchange, you will not harm our Nephilim or attempt to sway them toward a darker path."

Samael pursed his lips, watching his celestial siblings fidget uncomfortably. "You know, with a little training, I think my Sanura could best your coven." He smirked. "I'll pass." He evaporated, wasting no more time on idle threats, and reappeared beside the cypress tree near the cemetery—the place where his mate's soul called to him like a beacon.

Sanura stepped out and rushed forward, throwing herself into his arms.

He wrapped her in his tight embrace, inhaling her decadently sweet, woody scent. "Bond with me," he whispered against her hair. "Bond with me, and we'll destroy them all."

Chapter 30

Sanura

Sanura released Ba'al, leaning back. She'd stayed long enough to see him grow so immensely large his dark crown nearly scraped the ceiling.

"What?"

"Bond with me," he said again. "You are already mine. Let me share my power with you, and together, we will be unstoppable."

His words were intoxicating, and the blood he'd shared, still working to heal her ravaged body, zinged through her, charging her. Could there be more? More power, more strength?

"Who were the other creatures in the temple?"

Ba'al's lips lifted at the corners. "My siblings. Dina, Raphael, Sariel and Aniel."

She pursed her lips, marveling at their smoothness after being chapped and burned. "Why are you at odds with them?"

"For the same reason you're at odds with your coven. I'm different."

She studied his beautiful face, so unchanged, though so much was different from the man he'd posed as all those months ago when they'd met in her village under the cover of darkness.

"Did you know about me?" she asked. "Is that why you were with the king?"

Ba'al wrapped his arms more tightly around her. "No, my love. It was the happiest accident of my eternity."

"Then you are in service to the King of Israel?"

He barked a laugh, loosening his hold on her. "I am in service to no one. I am king of a realm far greater than this one, and when we are bonded, you will be queen at my side."

Sanura's chest hummed in delight, but his words were too sweet. Promises given too freely. If she had learned anything in this life, it was that no one could be trusted when a thing seemed too good to be true.

I would not deceive you, my light in the dark, my morning star.

Sanura gasped and pressed her hands to his chest. This close, she couldn't think of anything but him and those long fingers wrapped around her waist. Her mind swam with thoughts of their night under this very tree, though what she wanted now wasn't pleasure.

"Please, Ba'al. Let me go."

He released her easily, and she stumbled backward. Sanura turned, pacing away from him. The warmth living inside her tugged her to turn around, throw herself into his arms, and never leave, but she didn't want security. She turned back. "I hate them."

Ba'al nodded.

"I want them to burn as I did."

His seductive lips tipped up.

"I want them to scream for their deaths as they writhe in pain and rue the day they ever crossed paths with me." She met his bright sapphire gaze and a thrill shot through her. "Will you help me take my revenge?"

His teeth gleamed in the moonlight as he gave her a wide smile. "It would be my honor."

"Then tell me what I must do."

Ba'al closed the distance between them once more and held out his hand. Sanura took it, feeling that same tug in her chest she did every time they touched.

"Bonding on the mortal plane will unlock your seraph side. It will give you far stronger magic. With it, you can raise an undead army to end them all."

Sanura's grip tightened around his fingers as she nodded.

"Hold tight, and no matter what, don't let go until I say, okay?"

A breath escaped her as immense power spilled from his hands, racing through her veins; when it reached her heart, their magic twining together, Sanura's chest expanded, something filling all the dark corners until a presence so overwhelming filled her that she thought she might burst from holding it in. She gritted her teeth against the rise of voices from the ground, shouting, screaming. She squeezed her eyes closed, digging her nails into Ba'al's skin, fighting to maintain control as it begged to be freed.

"Release it, Sanura. Don't tamp it down."

Her eyes flew open, and she met his bright, electric eyes, dancing with undiluted power. Exhaling a long breath, she loosened some of the hold on her gift, and the earth rocked underfoot.

"More, my star. Let it go!"

Sanura unraveled more of the tightly bound control, and specters erupted from their tombs, untethered, shooting into the sky. She ducked, pulling some of her control back.

Ba'al's grip tightened on hers. "I have you, my love. Do not fear them. Own them."

She swallowed, the ember in her chest—now whole in a way she never knew it could be—thrumming as it asked for permission to be released. She had never let her magic loose, fearful of what would happen if she gave it free rein. Now—for the first time she trusted Ba'al would catch her if she couldn't stand on her own.

Power exploded from her as she released her hold. A shock wave ripped from her body, shaking the cypress tree at Ba'al's back, sending several tombstones tumbling to the ground. In the distance, dogs barked, and the flickering lights of Athens winked out, casting the city into darkness.

Ba'al's sapphire eyes glowed brightly; his hold was unwavering as the power she had kept locked up for so long bled freely from her. For the first time in her life, Sanura could breathe. She looked up and smiled at the wispy creatures hovering overhead. They'd been freed of their bones. Given permission to leave the mortal vices they'd clung to behind. Now, if she willed it, they could pass on, but only if she let them. She was their queen, and they were hers to do with as she wished.

CHAPTER 31

Aesop

Aesop raced into a room at the back of the house and stopped beside the women crowded around their Pythia.

Dina appeared, and they parted for her. She knelt beside the too-pale woman and pressed a palm to her cheek. Searching their faces, she halted at his mother's. "Leontia, I would speak with you."

Leontia dipped her chin and followed Dina from the room.

Aesop trailed them, hugging the wall, and ducked out of sight behind long billowing sheets.

"She is already gone, my child."

"Please, you must do something," Leontia pleaded. "Her babe is not yet four months, and she has no one to care for it."

"I cannot revive the dead, Leontia. She rests in Heaven now. Aniel will look after her soul."

His mother let out a small sob, and Dina leaned close to wrap a comforting arm around her. From his vantage point, Aesop didn't think Dina was particularly upset that Kassandra was gone. But his mother sagged in the angel's arms; her grief was perhaps enough for both of them.

"And Lysander? Has he gone home?"

Dina's snowy brow furrowed. "No, child. Lysander does not dwell in my realm."

Leontia gave a small yelp before she threw her hand over her mouth to cover the sound. She was always covering her grief and her pain, hiding it from them all in some effort to shield them. But she knew as well as the rest that they could smell it.

"Leontia, it was unwise to injure Sanura. I told you what she is to him," Dina continued. "He will not be satisfied with the death of your Pythia. I fear he won't be satisfied until he has wiped out the lot of you."

Aesop's mother narrowed her eyes. "She killed him. Aesop saw it. Should she go unpunished simply because she is the devil's mistress?"

"I do not believe she did."

"Aesop?"

Aesop spun around and looked up to meet Georgios' stern gaze. His brother grabbed him by his tunic and hauled him up.

"What have I told you about spying?"

Aesop scrambled out of his tunic, running nude through the courtyard, leaving his brother bellowing after him. He stopped in the staff's washing room and tugged a new too-large tunic off drying twine, slipping it over his head.

Georgios called out again, and Aesop darted behind a door and pressed himself tightly against the wall. He threw up a quick air shield, leaving only a tiny crack to hear sounds while muffling most of his own.

"Aesop. Come out and take your punishment," Georgios's muted voice yelled into the room. His heavy steps kicked up dirt as he shuffled in and began rummaging through piles of clothes. "A man accepts responsibility." Georgios picked up a crate and shook it out. "He doesn't run from it." He gave the room another once over before marching out.

Aesop waited a few moments, then let his bubble drop. He exhaled, waiting for any other sounds or smells of life. When he was sure no one was near, he darted out from behind the door and through an arched frame at the back of the house used only by the staff.

Outside, the sun shone over high stalks of wheat. He slipped between them, holding his fingers out and running them along the stalks as he let out a deep sigh. Nature—away from the plotting, pain, and death surrounding his family—was the only place he felt at peace. He reached the edge of the field and slumped against the bark of his favorite tree, peering up at the back of his house. From here, he could see into his mother's room, Helena's, and the one that had belonged to Sanura.

Something twisted in his gut. He had been wrong about her. She hadn't killed Lysander, and Aesop had been the reason they trapped her in that temple. If what Dina said was true—and it must be, for angels didn't lie, he had witnessed Sanura saving Lysander.

And he'd sentenced her to death.

CHAPTER 32

Sanura

S anura lifted both hands, and the earth shook.

"Very good, my love. Tell them what you want them to do."

She glanced nervously at Samael. The name was strange on her tongue, but now that they were bonded, his thoughts poured through her, and she could no longer think of him by anything other than the name he had given himself after his fall.

Sanura returned her focus to the spirits listlessly hovering around her. Lysander stepped closer but stopped when she frowned at him. Samael had released him from the cellar at the back of the Gavras home, and her heart swelled, knowing her lover had kept his promise. She felt a strange sort of motherly affection for her creature and couldn't bear the thought of parting with him.

"I can't focus on one at a time. I can only call them all," she said, sighing as Samael closed the distance between them and wrapped his arms around her. Her soul purred in response. Now, it did that every time they touched.

His lips grazed her ear. "Think of the way you called them before," he breathed against her lobe. "Pick out the one you want and give it a command."

A shudder rolled through her, and her skin tingled. "I can't focus on anything when you're doing *that*."

"You'll need to learn to control them when a dozen Nephilim come for you. And, my star, they will come. Now that they know about us, you won't be safe until they're dead." He nibbled her lobe. "This is a minor distraction compared with what you'll face when they attack." His lips skimmed the skin below her ear, and she gasped.

"I beg to differ." She spun around in his arms, her mouth finding his. Samael's grip loosened, long fingers sliding up her back to tangle in her hair.

Her heart raced as he wound her curls tightly in his grip, tipping her head back so he could deepen their kiss. Salacious, filthy thoughts poured into her mind, and she moaned around his mouth.

"Hi."

Lysander's words startled her, and she broke their kiss, cheeks heating.

"I don't like that."

She glanced at Lysander, who was standing uncomfortably close, then back to Samael. "What exactly did you do to him?" she asked.

Samael uncoiled his fingers from her hair, and they darkened at the ends.

"Don't hurt him. You promised."

He frowned, but his gaze remained fixed hungrily on her. "He's ruining our moment."

Sanura laughed. "I was supposed to be practicing."

Samael released her, hands trailing lightly down her back before he stepped back. "Very well. Resume your revenge training."

Sanura pursed her lips. "I may be doing this wrong. Lysander."

"Yes, my queen?" Lysander stepped around Samael, who narrowed his eyes at her creature.

"Your gifts differ from when you lived, do they not?" He nodded. "Are they the same as mine?"

"I don't know all your gifts, my queen."

She clicked her tongue. "Can you raise the dead?"

"No."

She twined her fingers together behind her back. "Give me a demonstration of your power."

Lysander raised both hands, and icy spikes shot from his palms, embedding themselves in a tree on the other side of the cemetery. He lowered his hands to the ground, where grass withered and died all around him. He stopped, crossing his arms over his chest. A smug smile played at the corners of his mouth.

"Is that it?"

His smile faltered. "I don't know yet. I can't burn things, but I can extinguish flame."

"Oh." Sanura uncrossed her arms. "That could be very helpful." She turned back to Samael with a smirk.

"What if, rather than creating an army of skeletons, I created an army like him?"

CHAPTER 33

Aesop

Aesop heard them approaching and scrambled around the tree trunk, poking his head out as Helena and her angel stopped in the field of wheat.

"He's going to force me to marry him, Aniel," Helena said. "I have to leave with you. I won't give him my body."

"I do not live on the mortal plane, my dove. You cannot come with me until death."

Helena beat her fists against his chest. "Is this what you want, then? For me to be another man's whore?"

Aniel wrapped his arms around her even as she wriggled in his grip. "Of course not. But I would give anything to allow you this one mortal life."

"I don't want it. I hate it here. I want to be with you. In Alaxia."

Aniel dipped his head, resting his chin atop Helena's, and she let out a muffled cry. "One day, my dove. Talk to your mother. Convince her to allow you to join the church. Then you will never be required to marry."

Helena wriggled in his arms again, and this time he released her. She glared up at him, stomping her foot in the tall grass. "The church? In Israel? Are you mad? We are Greek through and through. My family would never allow such a thing."

"Your family knows the truth. What greater purpose than to give yourself in service to the church?"

"We are gentile. Have you forgotten?"

Aniel sighed and turned away from Helena. "No." He spun back to her, searching her face for a long moment. "I must go. We are preparing for Sanura and her mate. We have much to do to ensure your safety."

"Do you truly think she'll kill us?" Helena's voice cracked.

"She will try, but it is not her we fear. It is her soulmate."

Helena's eyes were round, and she swallowed, nodding once.

He pulled her into another embrace and disappeared.

Helena's gaze darted toward Aesop, and he ducked his head. He held his breath, listening for any sign she was approaching.

"Dina."

Aesop peeked out again as a new angel appeared in the field.

"Yes, Helena?"

"I've decided."

Dina stepped forward, gripping Helena's hands in hers. "Will you do it?"

"Yes."

Dina squeezed her fingers tightly. "What made you change your mind?"

"I can't marry Erasmos," Helena said. "My heart belongs to Aniel. I can't spend a mortal life waiting to be with him." She tugged her hands from Dina's and spun away from her.

Helena paced toward the house, swiping her hand, breaking stalks of wheat as she marched. She turned back. "We're all dead, anyway, aren't we?"

Dina's brows dipped, sorrow in her gaze. "I fear none of us are strong enough to stop him if he truly wishes to avenge her."

Helena dropped her chin, resignation etched into her features. "Tell me what I must do."

Dina turned toward Aesop, and he froze, knowing he was caught. "Aesop, come here, child."

Helena glowered at Aesop as he stood, dusting his knees, holding his chin high, and marching toward them. He looked up at Dina's silvery wings blocking the sun, and his lip quivered.

"Does Helena really have to die?" he asked.

Dina knelt, meeting his gaze. "She is doing a brave thing so the rest of you may live," she said. "But you must promise me you will not tell your mother."

Aesop's vision blurred.

"Can you do that for me?"

Aesop glanced at Helena, whose arms were crossed tightly over her chest and back to Dina. "Isn't there any other way?" His voice broke over the words, and he swallowed, trying to be brave as Lysander had told him to be, confident as Georgios always said, but feeling very small.

"I don't think there is."

He rubbed his eyes, blinking several times. "What about Mother?"

"Your mother will care for you and Georgios."

He nodded gravely. "I promise."

Dina stuck her hand in her pocket and fished out a white stone—twin to the one she'd given him before. "Take this. It will give you courage when fear urges you in the wrong direction."

He took it, the same crackle sparking in his fingertips as the first time she gave him a stone.

Dina stood, smoothing her tunic. "Helena, come with me. Let us discuss what must be done."

They left him alone, holding the stone and all his fear over what was to come.

CHAPTER 34

Sanura

S anura raised an eyebrow. "What did you say she's done?"

"It matters little, my love. She is a witch, and her gifts, transformed by yours, will be a weapon in the coming battle."

Sanura's stomach flipped. Samael said the same about the last four men; he had ended them, and she called them back. But there was something different about the terrified woman clutching the fabric of her tunic. She didn't look like a bad person, but neither had the witches who took her in, treated her as a family, and pretended to care for her.

"On your knees." Sanura's eyes narrowed on the woman flanked by Mazikin and Astaroth, Samael's two highest-ranking generals.

The woman sobbed and wrung her hands together, sinking down. "Please. Please, Lady. I have children. They need me."

Sanura's grin faltered, and she looked at Samael. "Perhaps we should spare her."

Samael raised a brow. "She knows too much. If you let her live, she'll run straight to your coven, and they will have the advantage."

Sanura eyed the woman.

"I wouldn't, Lady. I promise."

The bitterness coating Sanura's tongue made her snarl. "Lies. You all lie!" She turned to Mazikin. "Do it."

Faster than a lightning strike, Mazikin's tail whipped through the air, spearing the woman through the chest. She cried out once before her head slumped to the side. Mazikin raised her tail, lifting her lifeless body, and Sanura pressed her palms to the woman's still-warm skin.

"Return to your body to serve in my army. Retain your most basic abilities to think and reason, but do not remember who you were or what happened to you. You will obey my every command. Wake."

The woman's lids flew wide, and she heaved in a great breath, glancing down at the spike protruding from her chest, and let out a blood-curdling scream.

Mazikin dumped Sanura's new creature on the ground, sliding her tail free, and the woman held both hands to her chest, continuing to shriek.

"Stop screeching," Sanura seethed. The woman's cries abruptly shut off. All the terror she'd felt was painted on her face, mouth stretched into a silent scream. "It's not quite right."

Samael approached the woman, leaning down to stare into her eyes. "Perhaps the key is allowing them to keep memories of their life without remembering the moment of their death. Let's try again. Mazikin."

"No." Sanura held up a hand, halting Mazikin mid-strike. "We cannot win against a coven of Nephilim with a five-creature army. We will have more opportunities to practice. Lysander, please take her to stand with the others."

Lysander gave her a lopsided grin, and her heart warmed. He wasn't fixed, but her new commands had brought him closer to the man she'd met upon arrival. The man who had shown her kindness and meant it.

"Careful, my star," Samael said. "With thoughts like those, I might grow jealous."

A sharp spike of fear shot through her. He had kept his word and left Lysander unharmed, but a streak of darkness lived in her lover; his threats were never in jest. She steadied her breathing, aiming for a distraction. "Time for the next part of my plan."

Samael's sable robes shimmered as he paced away from her and turned back, raising a golden brow in question.

"We cannot live in the cemetery," Sanura said. "I'm still mortal. I need rest and food."

He nodded. "What did you have in mind?"

"We need a home. A place for our army to hide, but somewhere close enough that we can keep an eye on the Gravas family."

Samael grinned, glancing at his generals. "Go. Find a home suitable for your queen."

They bowed low and disappeared.

"They won't hurt anyone, will they?" Sanura asked.

"My love, there are no unoccupied homes in Athens," Samael explained. "They'll need to ensure the occupants vacate."

Something cold settled in Sanura's stomach. It was one thing to plan revenge on the people who tried to kill her, but her new creatures—made from witches Samael had sworn deserved punishment—and the humans who lived in whatever home he would make for her were caught in the middle. The stone in her stomach grew heavier.

Hearing the indecision in her thoughts, Samael approached, taking her hands in his and kissing their backs.

Her chest buzzed as it always did when they touched, and the untethered spirits hovering nearby grew louder. She flinched, tugging her hands free.

"There's one more thing," she said, glancing at the creatures standing idly beside the cypress tree. "I want to send Lysander back to the Gavras house. He will be our eyes and ears."

Samael frowned. "They'll never believe it. Have you seen how odd he acts?" He beckoned the creature and said, "Lysander, come here."

Lysander tripped over his feet, stumbling to reach them, but his vision was glazed. He had grown increasingly distant as the days passed, even with her new commands. Sanura feared it was as she first thought. Perhaps his mortal body could only sustain him for so long, and he was breaking down.

"Yes, my queen."

His tone was flat, eyes staring distantly at some fixed point. Sanura shuddered.

Samael rolled his eyes. "You see. The moment he leaves your side, he'll stand like a statue, ignoring them all."

Sanura waved a hand in front of Lysander's face, but his clouded expression didn't flinch. "When was the last time you ate, Lye...sander." Her gaze darted nervously to Samael and back.

"I had a rat this morning, my queen."

She grimaced. "Are you hungry now?"

"What I crave, I do not have permission to consume."

"Curious," Samael said, folding his arms over his chest.

"What do you crave?" Sanura asked.

"Human blood."

Samael barked a laugh, and two nesting pigeons took flight overhead.

"Human blood?" Sanura pursed her lips. "Like mine?"

"Don't even think about it," Samael growled. "Your blood is mine."

She cast another wary glance at him. "What about one of the other soldiers?"

"They don't have what I need."

"Don't they?"

Lysander shook his head.

"Lysander, I give you leave to go find blood."

Before she'd finished speaking, he darted into the darkness so fast her hair whipped across her face.

CHAPTER 35

Sanura

S anura shuddered, wondering if she had just condemned some innocent human to death. What had she done to Lysander to make him crave blood?

"It's not the blood he truly desires," Samael said, hearing her thoughts. "He craves the soul's essence that he siphons from it."

Sanura's lips parted with a gasp. "I fear he'll kill to get what he needs from the humans."

Samael stood, closing the distance between them, and tipped her chin up. "They don't matter."

Her brow furrowed as their eyes met, and he ran a finger over her forehead, smoothing the crease. He pressed his mouth to hers—softly, reverently—and she melted into his touch. When their kiss broke, Samael's hungry gaze told her he wanted so much more. The ember in her chest pulsed, igniting her with new desire.

"My king."

Sanura started, her gaze shifting to Mazikin.

Samael's finger slipped from Sanura's chin. "Yes, number two?" His words held enough venom that Sanura flinched, even though they weren't directed at her.

Mazikin took a step back, glancing between the pair before she went on. "Your queen's home is prepared."

The blow came so quickly that Sanura had no time to prepare.

Samael's talons swung at his general, digging into Mazikin's chest. He lifted her off the ground, pulling her up to eye level, and his bright sapphire eyes gleamed with malice. His canines lengthened as his mouth opened. "She is *your* queen. Never forget that." The words were a low growl, deadly, and dipped in poison.

"Yes... my king." Mazikin turned toward Sanura, grimacing in pain as Samael's talons sliced deeper. "A thousand apologies, my queen," she said in a breathless gasp as Samael tightened his hold and squeezed.

As his talons closed around something dark within her chest, coated in green blood, Mazikin cried out but made no move to fight. Samael ripped the thing free and tossed it to the ground. She fell to her knees, panting, but to Sanura's horror, she didn't die.

Samael lifted taloned fingers smeared in Mazikin's blood to his lips and licked, his forked tongue sliding along the edges of sharp nails.

Terror shot through Sanura as she watched the scene, but her voice was gone—the air punched from her lungs. It was brutal and terrible, and her mate seemed pleased with himself.

"Bow, number two, and beg your queen for reprieve."

Mazikin crawled on shaking hands and knees and dipped her head until it touched the ground at Sanura's feet. "P-p-please... my queen... show mercy."

Sanura sank to her knees. "Yes, Mazikin. I forgive you," she said, her voice cracking.

"My love," Samael crooned. "Do not stoop for the creatures who serve you."

Mazikin whimpered, and Sanura laid a gentle hand on the flinching demon's back before rising to her feet. Her eyes narrowed on her mate. "Samael, why are you so cruel? She doesn't deserve this."

Samael's eyes widened, but in a moment, he grinned. "Mercy from your queen," he said, eyes never wavering from Sanura's.

He moved again, too fast for Sanura to track, and twisted the demon's head.

Mazikin slid through his fingers and disappeared.

"What did you do?" Sanura shouted, dropping to her knees and laying a hand on the darkened earth where Mazikin's blood still soaked it.

Samael knelt beside her, gripping her arm and lifting her. "I gave her mercy, my love. I banished her to Primoria, where she'll be restored, and the pain will be gone." Lifting her palm to his mouth, he ran his tongue over her skin, licking it clean. "Careful. Her blood burns your mortal form."

Sanura snatched her hand back, a war raging inside her. He had acted so viciously toward his soldier, but when she did as he asked, he'd released her from the pain.

Astaroth, Samael's number one, appeared. "I will prepare a bath for our queen," he said, dipping his head until it nearly reached the dirt.

"Come, my star, you need food and rest."

CHAPTER 36

Aesop

Aesop slipped behind a vendor's stand, watching Lysander wrap his arms around a woman he didn't recognize. He hadn't seen his brother since the night Sanura tried to save him at the festival, and his stomach flipped as he watched him now.

Lysander fell easily. A pretty smile or a shock of long auburn hair, and he was besotted. But it had been different with Sanura; his interest in her bordered on obsession. To see him with someone new so quickly surprised Aesop. At least he could bring good news to Mother. She desperately needed it.

Lysander's head snapped up unnaturally fast, and Aesop ducked out of sight.

He held still, listening for sounds he'd been caught. A prickle of apprehension ran through him, and he looked up, stumbling backward as Lysander's bright eyes stared down at him.

"Lye?" he asked, voice trembling.

Lysander said nothing, unblinking, his red lips resting in a thin line.

Aesop remained frozen, fear drenching itself over him like a blanket.

His brother's head jerked to the left in that same unnatural way, and he was gone.

Aesop sucked in several shallow breaths, heart beating a frantic rhythm in his chest.

When no sound came again for some time, he crept out of his hiding place and peered around the empty market. At this hour, the vendors had not yet begun to set up for the day, and the eerie silence permeating the pre-dawn market sent a chill of foreboding down his spine. Racing up the path to his home, Aesop dashed through the archway and into his courtyard.

Noise to his right had him sliding to a halt, and he flung himself against the stone. The strange sucking sound continued. It reminded him of the times he found Father in the storage room, slurping ale from the barrel after the rest of the house was asleep.

Hugging the wall outside the kitchen, he risked a glance into the room and gasped.

A dark figure hunched over Agetha's limp form.

Aesop held his breath as inhuman, glowing eyes shot up, staring directly at him. In the dark, Aesop could just make out the outline of Lysander's sharp jaw and his normally slicked-back hair falling across his face.

Lysander wiped a hand over his mouth, staining it red, and his fingers twitched.

Aesop pushed off the wall, running as fast as his legs would carry him to his mother's room. He reached her door and pounded. "Mother, Mother! Let me in!"

Her door flew wide, and Aesop tumbled to the floor.

"Aesop? What's wrong?"

Bracing both hands on the wood, he got to his feet and shoved the door closed, sliding the drawbar into place while heaving in great gulping breaths. "It's Lysander," Aesop said. "He's a beast!"

Leontia's hand went to her chest. "Lysander is here?" She pushed Aesop aside, raising the drawbar.

"No, Mother! Don't go out there. He's done something to Agetha."

Ignoring him, Leontia flung her door open and darted into the hall. "Lysander? My son, are you here?"

The desperation in her voice sliced through Aesop's chest. He ran after her, begging her not to go, but she took the stairs two at a time, calling Lysander's name again and again.

Aesop slid to a stop beside her as she froze in the doorway to the kitchen. Agetha lay sprawled across the counter, eyes wide and staring at nothing. He reached for his mother's hand to still his own from trembling, but she tugged her fingers free and turned from the gruesome scene, tearing through the courtyard, shouting for Lysander.

Aesop ran to the archway, wrapping his arms around himself as frigid night air settled in his limbs. His mother's cries faded as the darkness swallowed her in its embrace. He stood for several minutes, waiting for her to return, but the inky night only stretched on, smothering the few stars peeking through and devouring the moon.

As he turned back to the safety of his home, something caught his eye in the neighboring second-floor window, and he squinted into the blackness. Hairs rose on the back of Aesop's neck. Leontia's shouts should have roused their closest neighbors from their beds, but nothing stirred. A chill shot through him, warning him of more horrors yet to come, and he backed up, hugging himself tighter.

Inside, he climbed the stairs and knocked on Helena's door.

"Just a second," she called. Shuffling began behind the door, and something loud scraped against the wood. After an eternity, it cracked open, and she peeked out. "Yes?"

"Helena, come quick," Aesop said. "Lysander killed Agetha, and Mother went after him. We have to stop her."

Helena's puffy eyes went round. "Show me."

CHAPTER 37

Sanura

Sanura stepped back, melting into the shadows of her second-story window as Aesop's gaze scanned the space. He always seemed to see more than the rest, but it mattered little. Soon, they would all be dead.

Arms wrapped around her, and she stiffened.

Sanura couldn't deny the magnetism between her and the being who called her his queen, but his brutal outbursts toward those around him—those who *served* him—left a coldness settling in her bones. With her, he was gentle, but he tortured and killed others with no remorse. Was that what it meant to be an immortal being? Did a conscious only come with humanity?

She might have asked Helena, having an angel lover of her own. But Helena had betrayed her. A murky haze of red settled over Sanura's vision as she thought of the night they'd planned to burn her alive.

Samael's grip loosened, and he brushed her hair back from her face, running his lips down her ear to her steady thrumming heartbeat along the vein in her neck. "My love, I only want them to worship you as I do." His lips brushed her skin again. "You're a goddess. They should all kneel for you."

The ember in her chest hummed in contentment, preening over his fond words. In a world where only men were applauded for their strength and women who showed any spark of defiance were beaten until they dimmed, Sanura allowed herself to imagine the picture her mate painted. Could a world where women were treated as equals truly ever exist?

A door slammed below, disturbing the unnatural stillness permeating the space where her new army stood motionless, awaiting her commands.

She wriggled in Samael's loose grasp, moving to the door.

Lysander appeared in it, eyes alive in a way they hadn't been when he'd left earlier that night. "My queen," he said, bowing in the doorframe.

Samael's murmur of approval loosened some of the tension in her.

"You seem much improved, Lysander," she said.

He stood to his full height and grinned, bits of red gore stuck in his teeth.

Sanura hid her grimace. "Did you kill them?"

His grin fell. "Are you unhappy with me, my queen?"

She pursed her lips. "How many died? Who were they?"

Lysander's gaze moved to Samael for the first time, suggesting some of his faculties had truly returned to him, and it sent a wave of joy through her. Perhaps her creature would survive if he continued to feed on humans. Her chest warmed. Their lives for his. It was a trade she would accept.

"I took four lives," Lysander slid his tongue over a tooth, cleaning it. "Three coven members who attempted to kill you, and the housekeeper, Agetha, who shared your secrets."

Sanura inhaled sharply. He hadn't selected his victims at random; each act had been for *her*. Even in his nearly mindless state, he'd killed for her, sparing the innocent.

She turned to Samael. "The others will need to eat."

"Lysander." Samael's smooth tone was like honey as he glided past Sanura. "Are you prepared to serve your queen with a vital task?"

Lysander nodded eagerly, and Sanura's chest swelled. He hadn't acknowledged Samael before. Her creature was coming back to himself.

"Good. We need you to return to the Gavras home and report anything that happens there back to us."

Lysander pivoted on his toes.

"But."

The word froze him.

"You cannot kill any members of your family," Samael continued. "Those kills belong to your queen."

Lysander frowned, gaze shifting back to Sanura. "What about Aesop?"

Sanura opened her mouth, but her mate spoke first. "The boy won't be harmed."

The lie tasted bitter in Sanura's mouth, but she didn't intend to harm him and resolved to ensure Samael kept that promise. The women in that house had betrayed her, but the child was innocent.

Lysander nodded again. "I'll do it."

Her brow wrinkled. His consent was new, perhaps because Samael gave the order instead of her. She watched him go, moving so fast he was gone in a blink. Her gaze flicked to Samael as he paced her new room.

He turned back to her. "My love, I must see to a few things. I will leave you with Mazikin."

Sanura smiled. She relished a bit of space from the man who had jumbled her thoughts and at the chance to speak with Mazikin. To apologize.

Samael's brows slashed downward, a wrinkle forming in his brow, and he crossed the room, taking her hands in his.

"I know you think my actions harsh, but the demons only understand violence," he said. "If you give them an ounce of empathy, they'll use it to their advantage." He tugged her closer, and Sanura went, their bond lighting up as he wrapped his arms around her. His head tilted, resting on her shoulder. "Mazikin will guard you faithfully now, but only because I showed her what happens if she fails. It's the only language they know."

Sanura bit back her reply. Perhaps he was right. What did *she* know of ruling demons?

Samael leaned back, squeezing her fingers as he searched her face. "Say the word, and I'll put off my tasks and remain here with you. Your happiness is all that matters to me."

Something in Sanura's chest cracked, the resentment she'd been holding close falling away to reveal a heart that beat only for him. "Go," she whispered. "I need rest, and Primoria needs you."

He pressed a soft kiss to her lips, and she leaned into it, her eyes falling closed. When she opened them, he was gone.

CHAPTER 38

Helena

Helena's lips parted as she stared at Agetha's gaping mouth and cloudy, vacant eyes. She crossed the room in two long strides and pressed her hand to the woman's chest. Nothing. "Lysander did this?" she asked.

Aesop nodded, and his hand snaked out, reaching for hers. She curled her fingers around his smaller ones, squeezing.

"Why?" Her voice sounded hollow to her ears. Disbelieving.

"She wasn't the only one," Aesop said. "He killed a woman at the market, too."

Helena's gaze shot to Aesop's. "Who?"

He lifted a shoulder. "I didn't see her face."

She tightened her grip and turned from the room, pulling him with her. A child didn't need to witness such terrible things. "Where's Mother?"

Aesop stumbled as they moved, and Helena slowed her pace. She glanced back at his pale face and the dark circles under his eyes. Stopping, she knelt and threw her arms around him. "I'm so sorry you saw that, Aesop."

"Hey."

Helena shot to her feet, pushing Aesop behind her as she faced Lysander. He took a step toward her, but she threw out a hand. "Don't come any closer!"

Lysander shook his palms at her in surrender. "Helena, it's me."

Her brow quirked as she studied him. He was the same... but somehow *different*. His eyes were oddly bright, but that confident smirk he always wore played at the corners of his lips. Could Aesop have misunderstood the situation? He'd thought Sanura killed Lysander, but her brother was very much alive. Perhaps he'd gotten it wrong with Agetha, too.

"Where have you been?" she asked.

Lysander's arms fell to his sides, and his shoulders slumped. "Searching for Sanura."

The words were like a slap to the face as images of Sanura's charred body raced through Helena's mind. They were chased by visions of the angel who'd killed Kassandra, and she shuddered. "Why?"

Her brother's mouth puckered as if the question tasted foul to him. "What do you mean, why? You tried to kill her."

A tug on Helena's hand had her glancing back to Aesop, whose eyes had gone wide with terror as he shook his head vigorously.

Helena attempted a reassuring smile, but the hairs on her arms had risen; she sensed the same danger Aesop had. Surely not from her own brother. "Did you find her?" she asked.

Lysander smiled, but it was all wrong on his face, sharp angles carving his cheekbones into points in the dim courtyard. "Yes."

"And?"

"She's well. No thanks to you and Mother." His gaze swiveled left and right, peering into the dark corners of the courtyard. "Speaking of which, where is Leontia?"

Fear speared through Helena. Lysander had never called his mother by her name, and the gleam in his eye that promised retribution turned her stomach. Perhaps Aesop had not been wrong about what he'd seen.

"I'm not sure," she said hesitantly, tightening her grip on Aesop's hand in warning.

Lysander cocked a brow, giving her a dismissive once over before he marched past them.

She held her breath, spinning to keep Aesop behind her as he went. When Lysander was gone, she turned, facing Aesop.

"I'm going to get Dina," she said. "Find a place to hide."

His lip trembled, but his chin jutted out as he nodded.

Helena raced down the path toward their temple and up the steps, falling to her knees at Dina's marble bust. "Dina, I need you!"

The angel appeared, landing lightly and holding out a hand. "What is it, my child?"

Helena took it, pulling herself up. "It's Lysander. He may have killed people. Sanura did something to him. I don't know what, but he's home, and I fear for the family. The sooner we kill Sanura, the better."

Dina nodded, powder-white brows knotting between her eyes. "Come with me."

Helena followed the angel through the secret passage and down the stairs into the darkened room where no one had set foot since the night Sanura had nearly died. She tossed her flame to the rope ringing the room and set it ablaze as she raced after Dina. They stopped at the dais, blackened at the edges and coated in dark, dried blood.

Dina produced a gold coin from her pocket. "This will bind her. You cannot simply kill a necromancer. You must trap her so she cannot return. When you kill her, burn the body, but save a bit of bone—only a small piece—and melt the gold around it."

Helena stretched out her hand, feeling the weight of the cold metal as it landed in her palm. "How can I kill her? Her mate will destroy us before we ever get the chance."

"Leave it to us to distract Samael long enough for you to end her. But Helena, this magic requires sacrifice," Dina said, closing her hand over Helena's and squeezing. "You will be required to give your life."

Helena knew that. Had known what it would take and was prepared for it. She nodded, swallowing the terror rising in her.

"But first, you need a power boost."

Leontia appeared from the darkness, and Helena cried out as pain sliced through her middle. She glanced down, touching her fingers to the bit of metal glinting in the darkness, protruding from her stomach.

"Mother?" She sank to her knees, panting as she tugged at the blade handle. Bile rose in her throat, and she released it, lifting her sticky, wet fingers to her face. "Why?"

Leontia's eyes were filled with anguish as she touched her cheek, running a gentle hand over wet skin. "To make you a reash."

CHAPTER 39

Sanura

S anura rose late in the day, the soft rays of sunset casting the room in glimmering shades of orange and red. She sighed, stretching her toes as she lay for a moment, enjoying a peace she hadn't felt in years. There was always something to fear before. The people in her village could discover her secrets and come with fire and swords to cut her whole family down; the witches in her new coven could discover her secrets; of course, Antyamos.

Now, with a mate more powerful than the other angels and an army ready to kill for her, she could breathe for the first time. It no longer mattered if they knew the truth. What could they do to her?

A knock came at her door, and she sat up. "Come in."

Mazikin stepped into the room and bowed so low her horns scraped the floor.

"Please, Mazikin, rise." Remembering Samael's earlier words, she bit her tongue before asking her not to bow. Samael's warning clanged through her mind. *Demons only understand violence. If you give them an ounce of empathy, they'll use it to their advantage.* Sanura was through with being walked all over. "Is a meal ready?"

Mazikin nodded. "Yes, my queen. We have prepared everything downstairs."

Sliding out of bed, Sanura reached for a thick robe—left by her new home's former occupants—and wrapped it tightly around herself. Since arriving in Athens, the days had slipped from humid to balmy, and the nights had grown cool. A chill settled in the air, clinging to her skin, and she shivered rubbing her

157

arms as she followed Mazikin, mindful of her poison-tipped tail swinging behind her.

Downstairs, Sanura's gaze drifted over a spread that rivaled the one she'd become accustomed to in the Gavras home. As it turned out, two of the women in her army had been cooks, and their skills had been put to great use.

She sat, glancing around at her creatures, standing like statues, staring at nothing. "Come, children, eat with me."

They moved inhumanly fast, sitting around a large table, and eating ravenously. She had yet to release them to hunt, and her stomach turned at the thought of how much death more than a dozen creatures might bring, but Lysander's recovery had warmed a part of her soul and she could not watch the rest of her children suffer.

"Children." They looked up, glowing eyes fixed on her. "Tonight, I want you to feed, but don't kill the humans you bleed."

Mazikin dropped to one knee beside her. "My queen. If they allow the humans to live, they'll tell the others in town what has happened. It would lead to riots. You are safest if they kill them and remove their bodies."

Sanura studied the demon whose head was tipped to the floor, not meeting her gaze. She bit her lip, considering. The death of so many unsettled her, but a riotous mob of bloodthirsty men, bent on ending her and her creatures would not be borne. She had lived in fear long enough and would not allow her children to do the same. She nodded to Mazikin and faced the table. "You heard her. You shall kill the humans but do not kill any more than you must to maintain your strength. And do not harm the young."

A door opened at the end of the hall, and Mazikin tensed before disappearing.

Sanura glanced through the arched doorway, heart rate increasing. Had her fears already come to fruition? Were the people in town at her doorstep?

Mazikin reappeared, followed quickly by Lysander as he raced into the room and sat beside her. In a move very similar to his former human one, he grabbed a bunch of grapes and began popping them into his mouth.

Sanura's mouth fell open as he leaned back in his chair. "Lye?"

His lips stretched into a grin, and he winked at her. "My queen."

The playful note in his tone sent butterflies fluttering through her belly.

When he'd swallowed all his grapes, he leaned forward. "The witches are in their secret sanctum. Now is the time to make our move."

CHAPTER 40

Sanura

Sanura dressed quickly as tendrils of her power slid off her. Tonight, she would build her army. Tomorrow, she would have revenge. She left her room, linking arms with Lysander. Mazikin refused to stay behind so the trio marched down the dirt path towards town.

Lysander knew where each of the women in their coven lived, but Sanura shook her head, straightening her spine. The witches who had wronged her didn't deserve a quick death. She wanted them to fear her approach, to cower as hundreds of her children converged and when she reached them, she wanted them to beg.

Lysander moved swiftly on silent feet, dragging people from their beds and laying them at her feet. They were witches who hadn't been invited to Leontia's exclusive coven and had nearly as much reason as she did to hate them. Sanura pressed her hands to each—letting them keep memories of the coven members who had wronged them—giving them commands before instructing them to wake and serve her.

She sent them out to feed immediately, only giving them two restrictions: no members of Dina's coven and no children.

Mazikin joined the hunt, a glint of predatory glee in her eyes as she inhabited humans and brought them to her.

A cold sweat broke out on Sanura's brow when a man fell at her feet, still alive, and begged for his life and the lives of his family. Mazikin had darted back into the fray, leaving the man for Sanura to deal with. Her fingers trembled as she lifted a knife in her sweaty palms and lifted it. Too long. She was taking too long, but the handle of her blade slipped between her fingers as she wrestled her indecision into submission.

The man stopped begging, eyeing her warily. He stood, and without a backward glance, ran for his home.

Lysander was on him in a moment, draining him dry, and Sanura inhaled sharply as he dragged the man back, tossing him roughly to the ground. This dark side of Lysander seemed to delight in his new role and together, with Mazikin, they brought the city to its knees before their queen.

Sanura hugged the city's edge, following a narrow path to the coast. She reached the sandy beach just before dawn and sank down, feeling rough granules roll under her palms. She had used a great deal of magic bringing back so many tonight, but the seemingly endless well within thrummed in anticipation. She could have turned them all in a night without being drained, but she didn't need to kill everyone. She only needed enough to ensure the witches got what they deserved.

A line of fire appeared along the horizon, piercing the night. Soon, it would be time, but for the day, she would rest.

Sanura retraced her steps to the house atop the hill. Outside, a buzzing hummed through her, drawing her away from the courtyard and back to the sloping cemetery where she had hidden a few nights ago. The buzz became a chorus of shouts and wails, and she steadied herself against their cries as she stopped beside the cypress tree, resting her hand on the wood and letting out a small whimper.

Her gaze swept over a scene that turned her stomach. She bent, retching the contents of her earlier meal. Taking a few steadying breaths, she straightened and forced herself to look.

Limbs, twisted at odd angles, bent around one another, eyes staring at nothing. Bloodless faces, frozen in shock, peeked from between others, nearly unrecognizable as the bloodlust had taken some of her children when they fed. She'd made them wait too long, and the ravaged necks and shoulders of these humans told a story of their desperate hunger.

Staring at the mangled bodies below and the souls that clung to them or hovered nearby, Sanura was hit with the urge to keep them, to protect them from a final death.

She laid her hands on a body at the top of the pile and whispered the words that were becoming second nature.

He sat up, blinking. When his gaze met hers, he smiled.

CHAPTER 41

Aesop

Aesop wrapped his hands over his mouth to stifle a cry as Helena fell to the ground. His mother's tear-streaked face turned to Dina.

"Save her," she said. "You promised."

Dina nodded, and another angel appeared in the underground room. They held hands and began a chant that made the hairs on Aesop's arms rise as a hum began in his chest. A small blue wisp sailed upward, following a path of light until it disappeared. The new angel quickly touched Helena's lifeless form, a soft white light blooming between his fingers.

That humming in Aesop's chest grew stronger, and he felt an involuntary tug. It urged him to step forward and reveal himself to the angel with immense glowing wings, whiter than Dinas, but he remained hidden, feet firmly rooted in place.

When the angel lifted both palms from Aesop's sister, a soft glow emanated from her chest, and the two angels clasped hands again. A light burst between their arms as that same blue wisp traveled down its path, slipping into Helena's slack-jawed mouth.

She sucked in a great heaving breath, flying upright.

"What..." she said, staring around the room. "What happened?"

Dina produced a sword from some invisible place and ran her fingers down the blade, setting it alight. Presenting it to Helena, the other angel spoke, stealing Aesop's focus.

"You have chosen well, Helena Gavras. And for this, we shall bless you." Helena held up the flaming sword, staring at it, shock written plainly over her face. "Your sacrifice will mean a great deal to the humans." The angel's gaze darted to where Aesop hid behind a pillar. Something zinged through his chest before the being was gone, and cold emptiness washed over him.

"Your only chance will be when you get her alone. You're no match for the Fallen," Dina said to Helena.

Helena touched the middle of her forehead. "I feel... strange." Her gaze shot to the corner where Aesop was hiding. "Aesop!"

He jolted, freezing in place.

"Aesop, come out."

Slowly, he stood and stepped into the light.

Leontia, who'd been watching the scene mutely, sucked in a shocked breath and rushed forward, wrapping her arms around him. She brushed his hair back from his face. "Have you been hiding here the whole time?" she chided. "That wasn't meant for your eyes."

Leontia shuffled him toward Helena and he moved on numb feet, an electric shock zinging in the air.

Helena's outline glowed faintly, and her eyes were brighter somehow. She was his sister, but she wasn't.

The flames engulfing the sword winked out as he approached, and Helena rested a hand on her hip. "Aesop. I told you to hide at the house."

He blinked up at his sister. "I was, but..." His gaze darted to the stairs as if the creatures he'd seen might burst through the secret entrance at any moment. "They're killing everyone."

Leontia's grip tightened on Aesop's shoulders as Helena traded glances with their mother.

"I have to stop her, Mother."

Leontia nodded, dipping her gaze to Aesop's. "Stay here, Aesop. Do not leave this room until I return for you." Her eyes bored into his as she said, "I mean it."

He nodded, and the two women raced up the stairs.

CHAPTER 42

Samael

Samael paced the dark corridors of his underground Labyrinth. Guarding his realm had never been an issue. None of his brethren were truly selfless enough to risk their sanctity to curb his power, but Aniel wasn't like the rest. If any other possessed the same devotion to righting the injustices of their father, it might have been him. Only he had ever been selfless enough to put something or someone above his own eternity.

Astaroth appeared before him and dipped his head to the cold stone floor.

"Yes, yes," Samael said. "Rise. Speak."

"He hasssn't breached the realm'sss divide yet, but he sssearchesss for a way in."

A low growl erupted from Samael's throat. Only the dark-eyed angel with wings white enough to blind a man would do something so reckless as to come to Primoria and destroy his throne. The seat of Samael's power acted as a conduit, funneling the energy of Primoria's souls into him, making him ten times more powerful than his siblings.

Destroying his throne would level the playing field, even if a second seraph in his realm would exponentially increase its power. Without the throne to channel the magic, it would be up for grabs from any of them, and instead of directing the energy into his chosen few, all the inhabitants of the realm would have the strength to transcend.

"Mind the weak places between planes and put every able-bodied demon to the task." Samael wrapped claw-tipped nails around Astaroth's throat, yanking him closer. "Do not let him through."

Astaroth's form shimmered in his attempt to escape Samael's hold, enraging him further. He let his nails lengthen, slicing through the vital parts of his second-in-command before he checked his anger. If his second had to regrow limbs, it would waste precious time he didn't have.

Samael's nails retracted, and he flung the demon to the floor. "Go. Do your job."

He paced away from Astaroth simpering on the ground before the sight of all his pitiful groveling incited new rage.

All of this was because of Helena. Aniel feared for his mate—as he should. Samael would see to it that Sanura *would* have her revenge. He would blacken the night sky and end every creature who interfered to give his soulmate the time she needed to peel Helena's flesh back and discover just how much her mortal form could take before it gave out.

A booming sound like meteorites striking the ground resounded off the walls, and the floor shook underfoot.

Samael raced to his throne, sliding into his seat and gripping the arms. Dark, delicious power surged into him. He drank it in, absorbing as much as his immortal form could hold. If Aniel breached the realm, he would be ready.

CHAPTER 43

Sanura

Sanura glanced over her shoulder, a grim smile playing across her lips. Behind her, her children fanned out, blanketing the land. They stepped between stones erected for the dead who rested there. Seeing their lifeless forms piled atop one another and knowing her children were responsible twisted her insides. But restoring them, resurrecting them from that place between worlds where souls waited, had set the world right again.

She had never felt more alive than she did now.

After bringing back more creatures than she could count, she expected to be drained, but the energy thrumming below the surface of her skin was a living thing. It poured off her, shaking the ground as dead things ached to be near.

She had waited two nights for Samael to return, but he never came.

The power pressing against the bounds of her skin begged to be used and she could wait no longer. Sliding her feet out of her sandals, she exhaled slowly as her feet connected with the earth. All the things below the surface raced toward her: animals decomposing in the dirt, bits of wood and plant life, seeds that never sprouted, and the bones of the dead, rattled underfoot. For once, she didn't stop them, didn't force the magic down. Sanura embraced it, feeling everything around her come to life.

The massive cypress tree at her back groaned, and she turned, eyes stretching toward the sky as spikes of brittle dead wood punched through the roots and trunk. It creaked and tipped, crashing to the ground in a heap.

A thrill shot through Sanura. In a battle between life and death, death reigned supreme.

She turned back to the road and marched. "Come, children. It's time."

Sanura reached the Gavras home as the sun dipped below the horizon and stopped, pressing a finger to her lips. Her army halted, frozen in place.

She stepped through the arched frame and into a silent courtyard. Listening for sounds of life moving behind walls, her gaze swept over the place she'd once called home, a dull ache settling within her. She had longed for nothing more than to be accepted here, and though Leontia, Helena, and even Aesop had made her feel welcome, their kindness was a facade. They never truly cared for her, and when they learned what she was, they tried to kill her for it.

Something moved in her periphery, and her gaze darted left.

Shoes peeked out from under heavy drapery along the wall. On silent feet, Sanura moved, tearing the curtain aside.

Aesop's round eyes peered up at her, horror painted across his face.

"Hello, Aesop."

He made to run, but she caught him by the shoulders, pinning him in place. "I won't hurt you," she said, and meant it. "I'm only looking for your sister and mother."

He stopped fighting and faced her, his small chin sticking out. "I'll never tell you where they are."

Sanura laughed at his bravado. "You're loyal. That's what I like about you. But I *will* find them, and I can't have you telling them where I am." She scanned the darkness beyond the courtyard. "Mazikin." The demon appeared, and Sanura dipped her chin to Aesop. "Watch him. Inhabit him if needed, but don't harm him."

Mazikin bowed low and held out a hand to Aesop.

The show of kindness warmed something in Sanura's chest. There was a kindness in the creature and she feared Samael had molded and shaped her until she learned to hide it.

Aesop glared at her outstretched hand, crossing his arms over his chest. "I know what you are, demon."

Something like hurt crossed Mazikin's features, and she let her hand drop.

Sanura left them, rejoining her army outside.

"They aren't here," she said. "Come on."

They marched down the path to the market. Those few residents who remained slammed doors as they approached. At the base of the steps to Dina's temple, Sanura stumbled to a halt when three enormous beings landed, blocking her path. She recognized them from the night Samael had saved her from her coven. The female stepped forward. Dina.

"Sanura," she said. "The members of my coven are under our protection. We will not let you pass."

Sanura pursed her lips. Samael had said they couldn't harm her if she weren't actively harming them. But creatures that size could bar her path without inflicting damage. "I only want to talk to my coven. They are *my coven*, after all. I deserve an answer for their treatment."

A male angel stepped forward, flanking Dina. "We taste your deception, analogous umbra to the Fallen, and we will not let you pass."

Around them, humans peeked from behind their carts or windows.

She smiled up at the three beings. "And if you must choose between your witches and the other humans; I wonder which you'll pick." She glanced at Lysander creeping up beside her. "Go, create a distraction."

Lysander nodded, and her children darted away. Screams filled the air, and Sanura smirked as all three mighty creatures' horrified gazes darted in every direction. The two males leaped into the air, drawing swords. Dina remained frozen for a moment before she took to the sky, leaving a path for Sanura.

Sanura raced up the steps to the temple, passing each of the carved images of the angels before she reached the wall, pressing the pattern to open it. Her children weren't with her, but the power humming along her veins gave her strength, and she wouldn't get another chance alone with them while the angels were distracted.

She bounded down the stairs, hairs on the back of her neck rising as it closed behind her. It was reminiscent of the last time she'd been here, and a shudder rolled through her. She pushed the memory to the back of her mind as bare feet slapped stone on her way down the stairs. It was dark, with no light illuminating the space. Without the gift of fire magic, she would have to hope the others were as blind in the darkness as she was.

She tripped over something hard, stumbling to the ground, and the cold bite of stone sliced into her knee. Pushing to her feet, she slowed, letting her other senses guide her as her vision never fully solidified in the pitch darkness.

"Helena," she called. "I know you're in here. Don't be afraid. I only want to talk."

A shuffling sound to her left had her blind-eyed gaze darting toward it, but it was too dark. She moved, curling her hands into fists at her side. Stone rattled along the wall, telling her she was getting closer, and she tugged with her magic, pulling a massive block free from where she'd heard the noise before. It hit the ground with a thud, and more shuffling sounds caught her ear. She continued jerking stones from the walls, sending them crashing down, whipping them toward the sounds of feet moving in the dark each time she heard them.

Blinding light seared her vision as someone shouted: "Now!"

Hands grabbed her roughly, heat searing into her skin as her arms were forced up. Her heart rate exploded in a frenzied beat as she yanked against their hold, pulling her hands back, but she wasn't fast enough. White hot pain exploded in her left hand as the light sliced downward in an arc, severing a pinky finger. The light winked out; only the glow of red-hot fingers digging into her arms and shoulders remained as they burned into her skin.

Sanura thrashed in their hold, throbbing pain lancing through her as she ripped one hand free to call on the stones.

Someone grunted as a boulder hit its mark, but other hands replaced those, intensifying the heat of their grip as they pinned her arms across her chest, boiling skin where they touched.

As they held her down, Sanura thrashed wildly, searching the dark for something dead to call on for aid. But they had taken precautions, as though they knew this day would come, and their success would depend on her inability to use her gift.

Terror shot through her as hands clamped tighter, and the white flame flared to life again, illuminating Helena's face. Her heart beat painfully in her chest, drowning out everything else. Drowning out the world.

"You would have killed them all," Helena said with something like regret in her sorrowful tone.

The flames barreled for her, heat licking her cheek and neck. Samael's beautiful face flashed in her mind and she opened her mouth to call for him, to beg him to save her. But her skin bubbled under the flame's intensity and her scream died in her throat as the world went dark.

CHAPTER 44

Aesop

Mazikin evaporated as quickly as she'd come, a moment of terror streaking over her face before she was gone.

Aesop raced from the courtyard, sandals slapping packed earth as he ran. He had to warn them, to tell them Sanura was coming before it was too late. His mother bade him promise he would stay in the temple, but after a full night there, when no one had returned, he went in search of them and curled up on his mother's bed at daybreak.

Now, he was glad he'd come home. He could find them and warn them she was coming.

He reached the market, a heavy stone settling in his belly. Everywhere he looked, red painted the landscape—inhumanly fast creatures with glowing eyes sunk their teeth into the humans cowering behind stands and carts. Seraphim swung their swords wildly, taking out three or four of the creatures at a time. Aesop scanned them all, searching for his mother, for Helena, but they were nowhere.

Golden sandals struck the earth, and the ground reverberated with their impact. Aesop shrank behind a cart, gripping its edges to still the trembling in his fingers as eyes, black as night, scanned them all. The angel's dark gaze landed on Aesop, boring into his very soul. The angel tucked the largest pair of silvery wings Aesop had ever seen behind his back as it turned in a slow circle in the center of the battle.

"Enough," he bellowed. All around them, Sanura's golden-eyed creatures scrambled off the dead humans, darting in every direction. They moved so fast that Aesop couldn't make out their features. But they weren't fast enough.

The angel of death swung his whip in a wide arc, taking out dozens of them. They were sliced in two where they stood, bloodless forms crumpling in piles to the ground. His fingers lit with blue flame, and he flung balls of flame at another group, drenching them in fire.

Dina dragged Raphael with her as they met the angel in the middle of the market, each drawing a weapon.

Sariel and Aniel appeared, glancing at their brethren. Aesop ducked low as more of Sanura's army scattered under the new angel's barrage of flames and his massive whip.

"He's coming," Aniel said.

Suddenly, the air crackled. Aesop held his breath, ducking lower as a new creature appeared, larger than the rest, but without wings. Instead, his fingers lengthened into black points dripping with green blood.

Sanura's mate.

"Where is she?!" he demanded.

Dina backed up, and Sariel and Aniel closed ranks around her, letting the largest angel shield them all.

The massive dark-eyed angel spoke. "Who do you seek, Fallen?"

"My analogous umbra!" Samura's mate demanded. "You've harmed her."

"I know not of what you speak. I've been given a new mission, and I'm here to fulfill it."

Sanura's mate let out a mirthless laugh. "Father tasked you with another great quest. Why am I not surprised that the mighty Gabriel was bestowed another honor? You always were his favorite. I'm afraid I won't let you finish your task this time. These are my soulmate's children."

"Your other half made these abominations?"

Sanura's mate grinned. His smile was deceptively beautiful. Though Aesop knew he was evil, his face was almost too exquisite to look upon. "She was sorely abused by our sister's coven. She is owed retribution and her children will see that she has it." He glanced down at his long black talons, lips stretching wider. "And I would deny her nothing."

The largest winged angel, Gabriel, slid a long spear from his belt. "Stand aside, Fallen."

Sanura's mate opened his mouth to reply but clutched his chest instead. His eyes went wide, and he sank to his knees. "No! Nooooooo!"

Aesop blinked at the strange scene. No one had attacked him. He had simply collapsed. Aesop blinked again, and he was gone.

Dina moved to Gabriel's side. "They've done it. They've killed her."

Gabriel frowned. "Why would you do such a thing to his soulmate?"

Dina glanced around them at the death and destruction coating every surface. Aesop followed her gaze, noticing all the creatures around them were still. Gabriel had killed several, but not all. Something had happened to them.

Aesop let out a small whimpering cry when he spied Lysander's unmoving form sprawled across a pile of humans. He lunged forward, but shouting from the top of the temple steps drew his focus, and he sagged into the cart when he spied his mother racing down the stairs.

She fell at Dina's feet. "Please, Dina. Bring her back." Her head dropped, and she moaned as Dina stooped and placed a hand on her head.

Aesop stumbled from his hiding place and dropped beside his mother, tugging uselessly at her arm. "Mother. Lysander—"

"Dina, I beg you," his mother cried.

"Do you have the medallion, Child?"

Leontia blinked up at the angel, brows furrowed.

"The gold Helena entombed her bone in before you completed the ritual?"

Leontia fished in her pocket and pulled out an oval-shaped bit of gold.

Dina's gaze shifted to Aesop.

His vision blurred as he looked up at her. His chest heaved as he struggled to suck in another breath. Had he lost both his siblings today? "Are they really gone?"

Dina nodded, handing him the golden object. "Your sister gave her life to protect this, Aesop, and now you must protect it with yours. If the Fallen were to retrieve it, it could be catastrophic for our line."

Aesop clasped cold metal in trembling fingers, fisting it tightly.

Shrieks filled the air as members of the coven raced out of the secret exit, falling at Dina's feet. "Dina! Dina, protect us!"

Aesop looked around for some new foe to face, but there was no one left alive but Dina, his mother, and the women falling at her feet.

Dina was quick to react, wrapping huge wings around them. "Has he returned? Is the Fallen here?"

"He was," one of the witches said through her tears. "He took her body, but Dina... she was with child. He's vowed to end us for killing his unborn babe."

Dina's wide-eyed gaze shot to Aesop. "He *will* bring her back. It's up to you now, Aesop."

Aesop clutched the golden amulet—forged in his sister's blood, housing the bone of his enemy—tightly. His shoulders straightened as he said a silent prayer, swearing on his family name and all who had died to ensure Sanura was ended that he would protect it. And one day, when he was stronger, older, he would raise his own army and end her for good himself.

CHAPTER 45

Sanura

Sanura blinked as she took in the frigid dark room. Her eyes adjusted quickly, but the cold bit into her skin. She lifted both hands, scanning their bluish pallor in the strange light. All the burn marks she'd endured were gone.

Gasping, her hands flew to her neck, and she groped her chin, ears, and hair, resting both hands on top of her head. She winced, holding out her right hand.

The pinky they had severed was still gone, but the rest of her had survived the attack.

But where was she? Glancing around the cold, dark space, she spied a stone chair, thrice the size of a normal one, centered across from a whirling vortex she had missed until now. She stood on shaky legs and moved toward it. Its pull whipped the air but didn't seem to affect her.

She approached, stretching out a hand. It rippled around her fingers, swallowing them, and she pulled back, cradling her hand to her chest.

"Sanura."

The dark, sensual curl of her name on his tongue had heat burning low in her belly as she spun and faced him. In this dim space, he glowed, ethereal as his golden outline shimmered against the onyx backdrop.

She rushed to him, throwing her arms around him.

Samael folded her in his embrace, resting his chin on the crown of her head as he leaned down and inhaled deeply. "I was afraid you would smell different here," he breathed against her hair.

She leaned back, tipping her head up. "What do you mean... *here*?"

Samael's strangely illuminated eyes brightened. "You are in my realm, my star."

She gasped, pushing out of his arms. "I'm dead? They killed me?" An edge of panic rode her words as she heaved in gasping lungfuls of air, but even as she worked through it, she didn't feel herself tipping over the edge. A sense of calm settled in her bones, unaffected by her fears. All at once, desolation gripped her. She had planned to teach them all a lesson. To show them she was so much more than they were, but Helena had bested her with that glowing sword.

Thinking back to her final moments, she saw how naive she had been, assuming she could take them all alone. They had their Pythia's visions and an army of angels on their side. All she'd had was her children, so untrained, and her mate.

She glared up at him. "Where were you? How could you let them kill me?"

Samael's mouth curled into a vicious snarl. "Do you think I would have let them take my unborn babe?"

Sanura's hands flew to her belly. "I was with child?"

Samael's brows dipped, mouth smoothing out as he pulled her close again. "Yes, my love. They stole him from us."

Sanura's anguish broke over a fury rising so fast she hardly knew what it was before it burst from her, and she screamed her rage. "Those bitches stole everything from me!"

Samael shushed her, rubbing circles on her back, but she wedged her arms into his chest, shoving him away. "Don't comfort me. Don't you dare! I want them to pay!" Ice, far colder than the air frosting her lungs, raced up her veins, piercing her heart. She gasped around the pain slicing through the dead organ, gritting her teeth. "I'm going back. I'll wipe their line from the face of the Earth." She faced Samael. "Will you help me?"

Samael held out a hand, and Sanura took it. He leaned down, pressing a kiss to her cold, bare knuckles. When he straightened, his lips stretched into a sharp smile. In the near-pitch darkness, his teeth gleamed. "If my star desires it, I'll burn down the world."

"No. I want to do it myself."

THE END

EPILOGUE

Aniel appeared in Alaxia and raced to the pearly gates, his heart swelling even as the pain of her loss tore his chest in two. He'd wished for nothing more than to bring her with him to Alaxia rather than allow her to wallow in her human life any longer, but such an act was too selfish for his human soulmate.

But fate, or her own stubborn actions, had taken her life early, and now she would spend eternity with him.

Others gathered at the gate, waiting with him, ready to witness as they bonded one final time, sealing their fates to one another forever.

Pain in his chest intensified, even across planes, but she didn't arrive.

Raphael wasn't there, still healing from his injuries, but that should not have deterred her from making her ascent.

Fear gripped him. What if she had not ascended? He shook the thought from his head. She was brave—selfless—sacrificing her own life to protect everyone else.

Pain lanced through him again, and he gasped, horror drenching him. *She's not dead yet.*

He fell back to Earth, back to the temple, and through the walls, dropping beside her and letting out a pained moan.

Helena's eyes fluttered open, and he lifted her head gently in his lap, agony wrenching another sob from his chest. She had lay here dying with no one to comfort her while he waited in Alaxia like some lovesick fool.

"I'm so sorry. So sorry." He dipped his forehead to hers, gasping around the pain as her breaths came excruciatingly slowly. He spread his palms wide, soft,

177

white light flaring to life under his palms and he tried desperately to push healing magic into a body drained of its lifeblood. "Damn Dina and her plans. I care not for any of it. Wake, my dove. Live."

Her hand found his and gripped it weakly as her lashes fluttered closed. Her heart thumped once more before her hand fell slack.

All at once, the vice-like grip around his chest loosened, and he tipped back his head, screaming his desperate anguish. The pain choked him, stealing his breath as tears streamed silently down his cheeks. Lifting her body to his chest, he wrapped her tightly in his arms, hugging her to him, wishing against everything he'd been there sooner to hold her through all that pain.

He carried her body up the steps, finding only Leontia left among the carnage. He laid her daughter at her feet, burning eyes meeting her red-rimmed ones.

She fell on her daughter, sobbing—lost to her own grief.

Shedding a final tear, he stood and disappeared from the mortal plane, reappearing in Alaxia.

Heaviness hung over him as he waited, the fear of reliving his earlier experience shooting through him and the guilt of leaving her to suffer alone. He watched the gate. It remained solidly closed. None of his siblings joined him. The moment stretched on in a place where time didn't exist, and Aniel's chest sank.

Zadkiel appeared beside him and said, "Brother. What is it?"

Aniel opened his mouth to speak, but his grief was lodged solidly in his throat, so he closed his mouth and shook his head. He'd been in the wrong place at the wrong time, and while he'd awaited her arrival, she had struggled for her final remaining breaths. When she arrived in Alaxia, he hadn't been here to greet her.

Helena's soul had carried through to the fields all humans remained in, awaiting the day Heaven and Earth would collide.

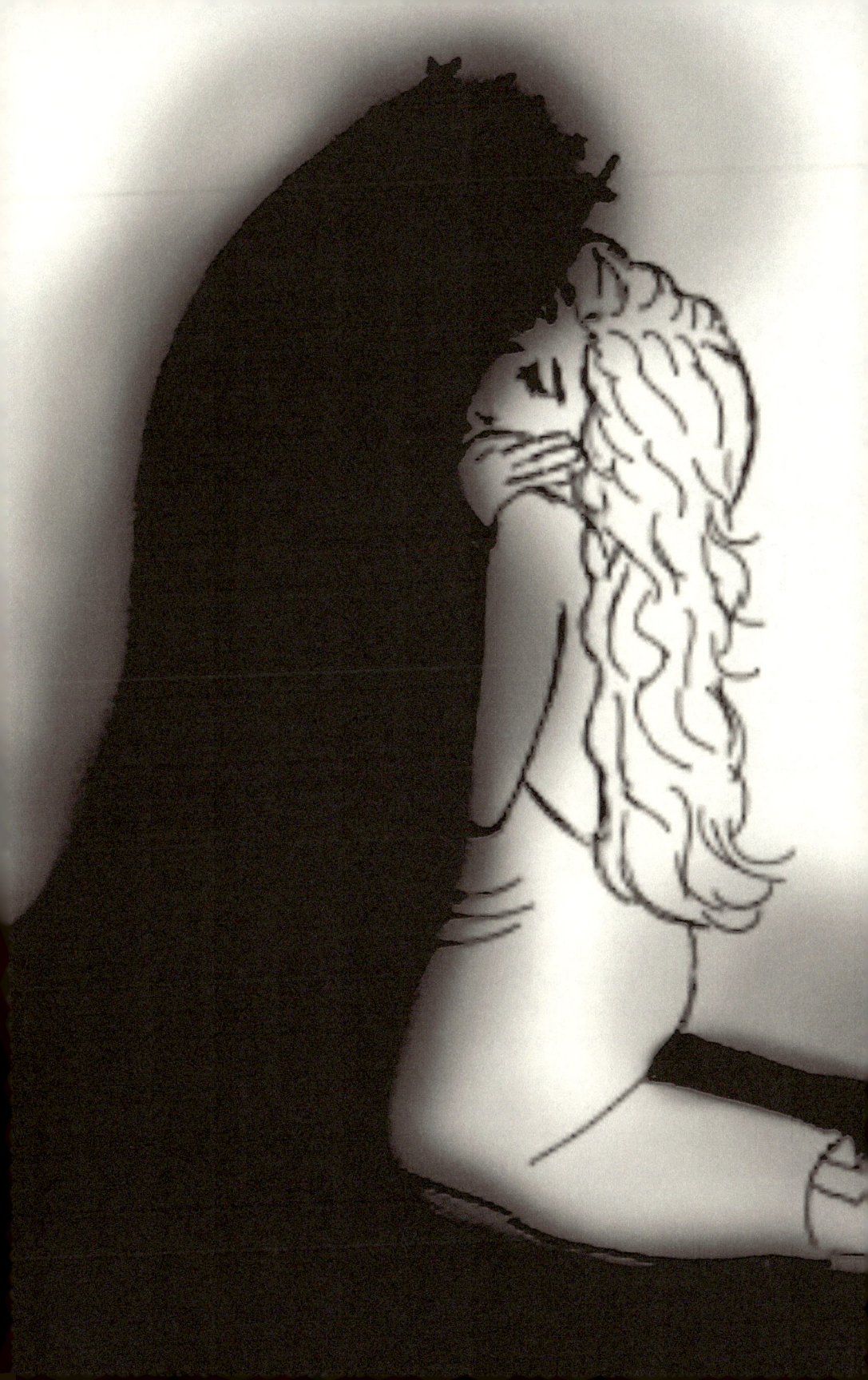

PARABLE PREVIEW

P rologue

This early preview of Parable is the unedited version. The final book may change drastically. Please note this book is intended to be read after book 3 – Grave Revelations. Spoilers follow.

Helena

Helena felt it before it happened. The static place she'd been in for some immeasurable period bloomed to life. It unfurled into awareness, then sensation, then a weighted heaviness that rooted her to the earth, centering her on one plane. Finally, blinding light as new eyes opened, and she turned.

Nothing mattered but the sight before her. It was her soul's reason for existence, her universe.

She ran, crashing into him and he caught her, lips melding with hers as they reunited in a beautiful moment. They were hands, lips—bodies—pressing closer, desiring nothing more than to consume one another; to become whole.

When they did, saying the sacred words that bound them together, Helena felt the rightness of it and knew no matter what she endured from now until the end of eternity, she could face it with Aniel by her side.

Hand in hand, they traversed a glittering rainbow of light refracting every known and unknown color of the universe, winding down a steep slope, but never slipping, never losing their way until their feet touched ground and Helena spun in a circle, wide-eyed.

"Where are we, my love?"

"This place is called Colorado," Aniel said, squeezing their laced fingers tightly. "We cannot go to Athens, Dove. It no longer exists."

There was a momentary heaviness in her chest, but it was chased swiftly away by the pulse of their soul filling her to bursting and she smiled up at him. "I will live wherever you are and wherever you are shall be home."

He smiled fondly at her, leaning down to kiss her forehead.

"Helena?"

She pulled back from Aniel's touch and stared up at a man at least a hand taller than her. "Yes?"

"Helena, it's me. Aesop."

Helena's hand tugged free from Aniel's as it flew to her mouth. "Aesop?" She let out a small cry and ran to him, wrapping him in a tight embrace. "But you're a man now!"

His stoic expression never faltered as she released him, leaning back to take him in. "You're so tall. Taller than Georgios. Taller even than Lysander, I think. Where are they? And mother? Are they here?"

Aesop's brows slid low, bunching at the center. "No."

"Why ever not? Isn't this the end of the world? I thought..." She trailed off, glancing at Aniel who wore the same somber expression her brother did. "Were they..."

"They were not welcome in Alaxia, my dove."

A sob bubbled up Helena's chest. Her mother. Her mother had been kind and fair. How had she not been welcome in Alaxia? And Lysander, sweet, generous Lysander had always looked out for others. She inhaled a long breath, trying to remember those last days of her human life, but memories were still filtering in.

She gasped. "Sanura. Is she..."

"Ended by our ancestor. You'll meet her," Aesop said.

An angel landed beside them and slid an arm around Aesop's waist. He was tall and lean with a self-assured expression that made Helena want to laugh, but the familiar way he was embracing her brother had her eyes narrowing. "Aesop. Who is this? A boyfriend? Are you old enough to date?"

The angel with his arm wrapped possessively around Aesop, snorted.

"Helena, I'm three thousand years old. This isn't my boyfriend. He's my soulmate and we've been together in Alaxia a long time. You were my older sister once, but my time has long surpassed yours and I am afraid you are the adolescent now."

"I'm Zadkiel," the angel said, holding out his free hand. "It's nice to meet you. I was overjoyed to learn Aniel's mate finally returned to him."

Helena stared at his outstretched hand, then up at his face. "Zadkiel... Do I... know you?"

He smiled. "We met once."

Aniel found her hand again, lacing their fingers together, and tugged her to him. The desire to be close—to touch—was overwhelming, and all her focus moved to the angel at her side. She inhaled his scent and sighed.

If anyone had asked her what the end would look like, she never would have predicted it would be this.

"Wait. Where's Dina?"

Chapter 1

Peter - Several days earlier

The ground rocked beneath Peter's feet, and shouts of dismay rose from the field of lavender as souls swayed. He scanned the distant horizon, searching for the cause of the disturbance, but saw nothing but an expanse of purple swaying lazily on an imaginary breeze.

Yesterday, the boats had stopped arriving and of the souls who remained in Sheol, there was a clear divide. Those who should have gone to Primoria were alert, anxious, and unsettled here. No amount of soothing earth magic funneled into the place seemed to put them at ease.

The other group listed aimlessly, swaying with the wind.

Until yesterday, some found their way to him every day, waking from some stupor, but when the boats stopped arriving, the souls had slipped further into a state of catatonia.

The ground rumbled again, and Peter blinked. Was the line of trees encircling the field closing in?

"Peter." Peter turned as Asher rushed to his side. "Peter," Asher's small cheeks puffed in and out. "It's starting. The realms are colliding."

A cold weight settled in Peter's stomach.

The ground shuddered again, and this time he knew he wasn't imagining it—the trees were much closer. The field had shrunk by half.

He glanced back at the sphinx. "What does it mean for us?"

Asher pawed the earth. "We'll be on Earth soon."

"What about the souls who were bound for Primoria?"

Asher's eyes widened. "They were meant to freeze in the icy depths of Primoria. Now that it's gone, I fear they will meet some new and terrible end when we arrive on Earth."

When the ground quaked this time, half the field was gone in a blink, and with it half the souls. Peter swallowed, searching for Cassia among them. His mind conjured souls reforming on Earth, only to find themselves spiked on shards of ice or trapped beneath frozen lakes.

He had to do something.

Dashing away from the sphinx, he stuffed his hand into his pocket, running a thumb over the crease marring the surface of the amulet he'd found laying on the ground moments before his death. He hadn't expected it to come with him to Sheol, but after so many years with it, it was a reassurance. A last comforting vestige of life on Earth.

Now he was returning to that place, but he wasn't sure what he would return to. Was Earth to be his new hell? Would he arrive there only to find himself trapped in some endless torture? Could he even die now that the world had ended?

His thumb rubbed a slow circle over smooth gold as it warmed under his touch, catching on the groove of a crescent moon. He stopped after at the banks of the river, mouth hanging open.

It had taken less time than usual to arrive, but what shocked him most was the massive crack zigzagging along the bed of a bone-dry riverbed. A distance that had always appeared hazy before, ended in a cliff of nothingness. Where the boat disappeared into some distant horizon, unreachable to the likes of him. A black void.

"Peter."

His gaze darted left. "Cassia. Where are the others?"

"Some have already disappeared."

He nodded. "Get whoever's left. Meet me back here as soon as you can, but don't waste time on those who don't want to come. We have to get out of here."

She dipped her chin, disappearing as quickly as she'd come.

Peter stepped into the dry riverbed, skirting the crack. He followed it, halting at cliff's edge, and glanced down.

The ground rocked as another tremor shook the earth, and he stepped back. Leaning forward, he searched the nothingness for any sign of life. With his normal human eyesight, he could see only blackness. Closing his eyes, he listened. Far in the distance, he heard... running water. Had the river sunk into some new realm?

Cassia appeared beside him and leaned to get a better look. "You can't be serious."

He glanced back, spying the gathered mass of souls behind her. "Is this it?"

"More disappear every minute."

He nodded. "What waits for us on Earth will be our reckoning. I'd rather take my chances with the void." He turned around, facing the crowd.

They pressed close to one another, glancing nervously at the blackness ahead, but many were darting looks over their shoulders at the shrinking mass of land behind them.

Peter lifted a hand. "I'm not asking any of you to come with me. But I will not wait for a punishment on Earth. I'd rather face a permanent end than an eternity of torture. But you must each make up your own mind."

Grumbling responses followed and when the ground rattled underfoot the next time, the nothingness coming for them closed in.

"I'm going. It's your decision." Not waiting for a reply, he turned, leaping off the cliff, and desperately hoped he had made the right choice.

FATED

Parable is coming February 2025.

THANK YOU

T hank you for reading Fated a Prophecies of Angels and Demons Novella. If you enjoyed this story, please consider leaving a review.

Amazon

Goodreads

ACKNOWLEDGEMENTS

You're reading this book for one of two reasons – You loved the series enough to read the novellas or you want a taste for the world of POAAD and you started here. Either way, I am so grateful you're here. I hope the story captured your attention and dragged you so far below you had to read the rest. Readers like you are the reason I continue to spend my Saturdays crafting characters and worlds. Writing a book is no easy task. It takes a village. This section is a special thank you to my village.

To my mom, as with the other books in the series, thank you so much for all your support and willingness to be my alpha reader through the entire series.

To my son, who is proud of his mom even if my second job takes time away from mom and son time.

To my street team for shouting about my story from the rooftops and encouraging other readers to take a chance on POAAD. This book deserves a special thank you to Trisha who had me double and triple checking facts to ensure she got the best possible story.

To my editor, Michaela Choi, thank you for everything. Without you, these books would be a mess!

To the artists who brought all the characters in this series to life. You mean the world to me.

To you, the reader, thank you so much for joining me on this journey. I hope the characters of the POAAD series live with you long after the books are finished.

Thank you.